HALLOWEEN PARTY 2017
MILTON WORKSHOP ANTHOLOGY SERIES
FALL 2017

DEVIL'S PARTY PRESS

ACKNOWLEDGMENTS

MILLER'S FACE. Copyright © 2017 William F. Crandell. Reprinted with permission of the author.

US 120 NORTH. Copyright © 2017 David W. Dutton. Reprinted with permission of the author.

...WARMER AND CLEARER TOMORROW. Copyright © 2017 David W. Dutton. Reprinted with permission of the author.

EL DÍA DE LOS ANGELITOS INOCENTES. Copyright © 2017 TJ Lewes. Reprinted with permission of the author.

A HOME FOR THE INCURABLES. Copyright © 2017 Bayne Northern. Reprinted with permission of the author.

BROTHERS LIKE NO OTHER. Copyright © 2017 Bayne Northern. Reprinted with permission of the author.

DEFUNCTS' DAY. Copyright © 2017 Dianne Pearce. Reprinted with permission of the author.

THE TRUCK. Copyright © 2017 Dianne Pearce. Reprinted with permission of the author.

DOORKNOB JESUS. Copyright © 2017 Mark Alan Polo. Reprinted with permission of the author.

THE TIBETAN ADDRESS BOOK OF THE DEAD. Copyright © 2017 Judith Speizer Crandell. Reprinted with permission of the author.

SKIN SUIT. Copyright © 2017 David Yurkovich. Reprinted with permission of the author.

CONTENTS

Milton! thou shouldst be living at this hour . . . Thou hadst a voice whose sound was like the sea . . .

LONDON, 1802
William Wordsworth

The charm of horror only tempts the strong.

Jean Lorrain

HALLOWEEN PARTY 2017

PREFACE

I FORMED THE MILTON WORKSHOP in March 2015. It started small, and has remained this way by design, as most good workshops do. When I first posted a member recruitment ad on the local Milton, DE, Facebook page and in merchant windows around town, I expected few responses. The ad featured a 1935 photo of Ernest Hemingway aboard his yacht, the Pilar, appearing to take aim at the viewer. To this image, I added a caption: *Join the Milton Workshop and finish your damn novel!* The threat was equally for me as for anyone who might join because, as much as I want to write, I need the "push" of a regular meeting to force me to find time for it in my life.

I was new to Milton; no one really knew me, and yet a handful intrepid souls arrived at my house on March 22, 2015, for our inaugural meeting. I admired their bravery, but didn't necessarily expect to admire their writing. I was very wrong on that count. As each author read his or her work, I thought, *Wow, that was really amazing!* I feel that the workshop, and especially I, have been incredibly lucky to find writers who are both very dedicated to their craft and exceptionally talented, right here in this little part of the world.

Being both brave and talented, you can expect these folks would also be ambitious, and you'd be correct. A few of us have formed a publishing house–the Devil's Party Press–a name chosen in homage to our patron saint, John Milton, who was said to belong to the Devil's party. It seems a perfect fit for the audacious souls who have been working together diligently now for almost three years to finish their damn novels.

The *Milton Workshop Anthology Series* was developed to showcase our efforts. For this debut issue, which includes work by most of our members, we chose to create a horror anthology, an idea that developed after the workshop members were assigned the task of submitting a story in the horror genre. The outcome may surprise you, particularly if your understanding of the genre is limited to the offerings of Hollywood. Within these pages are stories as diverse as the writers who penned them, with themes ranging from the supernatural to pure run-for-your-life-terror.

When horror fiction is mentioned, many think of the modern-day master of the macabre, Stephen King. Mr. King has a wonderful quotation about the writing process, which explains why the people in this book meet every two weeks no matter how busy our lives become:

> *Writing fiction, especially a long work of fiction, can be a difficult, lonely job; it's like crossing the Atlantic Ocean in a bathtub.*

So true.

Time now to break out your security blanket and join us in the bathtub for a terrifying ride across the ocean. We welcome you, but accept no responsibility for anyone who dies from fright!

DIANNE PEARCE
Milton, Delaware

MILLER'S FACE

William F. Crandell

IF MY SHIRT BUTTONS WERE thinner, I'd have been closer to the ground. Bullets burst around us. For most of fifteen minutes I could do nothing but memorize Miller's face. I can still see it.

We were eating lunch when the VC opened fire. A can of boned chicken lay splattered beside Miller. Its whitish-gray color, its terrifying motionlessness mocked his cheeks.

So Miller was alive. Not that it showed. Even his sweat stood still until the sun dried it.

His nostrils were flared. Miller risked making them bigger so the acrid air might wander into his lungs without any telltale breathing. His pale blue eyeballs were fastened on the three inches between Miller's locked fist and his rifle.

I saw no change in his face the whole time, except in the little creases between his eyebrows whenever a marine cried out. A steel helmet with a torn cover hid the top of his head, giving his scalp no more real protection than his jungle boots offered his drawn-up feet. His straight jaw was clenched, as if to steel him against the inevitable impact.

The bullet did most of its damage unseen, disappearing through a dime-sized dab of red at the base of his throat and tearing downward. Miller barely flinched. Then his eyes met mine just before they went dim, and every muscle relaxed.

I guess I was luckier. The battle didn't leave any marks on me that show.

BROTHERS LIKE NO OTHER

Bayne Northern

"SAMMY, I'M AFRAID! HOW DID we get here?" Sean was quivering. Shaking with fear. Sammy pulled his brother toward him, hugging him tightly against his barrel-shaped body.

"I don't know how we got in here. But we will figure out how to get out! " he promised, trying to make his voice sound confident.

Sammy was the older of the two. He felt responsible for his little brother. Sammy could hear his mother's voice reverberating in his head, telling him to watch his little brother while she quickly scampered toward the ocean, her legs sinking into the wet sand, anchoring her as a big wave crested and broke, the foam rolling up the steep shoreline.

"It's dark in here!" Sean began sobbing.

"Don't be afraid! Let's treat it like an adventure! Let's try to figure out where we are, even though we can't see anything. We can still *feel* things. Tell me what you feel!"

Sean pushed himself out of Sammy's grasp. "Well, it's wet and sandy, just like where we were before."

"Excellent! Keep up the good work!" Sammy encouraged his little brother while he tried to orient himself. "It's is a lot wetter than where we were before. And a lot darker. I can't see a single ray of sunlight."

"I just bumped into something hard."

"Hard?"

"Yeah. Like a wall. It's cool to the touch."

Sean placed his body against the damp exterior, feeling around for some kind of opening–a possible way out. He followed the hard surface, cautiously creeping step by step, reaching up as high as he could go and then down into the wetness below, but he couldn't find any gap in the enclosure. The shell-like façade surrounded them.

Suddenly, a big gush of water poured into the wet and sandy space carrying little bits of seashells and pebbles, almost drowning both of them.

"I think I see something red in here. I'm scared! Did we get swallowed by a whale?" Sean's voice rose to a high crescendo. "Are we going to die, Sammy? Inside a fish? Mommy will never find us!"

Sean's little, rotund body began to shake violently as he sobbed. Small bubbles appeared around his mouth each time he exhaled.

"I don't think we're inside a big fish. Together, we'll find our way out! We are big and brave–brothers like no other!"

Their familiar war cry. They always chanted it when they competed in a sport, usually swim meets. Sammy excelled at the free-style crawl. Sean usually won the breast stroke.

"Brothers like no other! From the same mother!" Sean yelled from the other side.

That made Sammy laugh. He loved his little brother. They were truly bonded to one another. They looked alike, both sporting rounded bellies, shorter than most of their friends and all of the girls. But both agile swimmers. Excellent sand castle builders. Adept at burrowing in the sand and burying one another within minutes.

Suddenly their dark, damp, sandy environment began to move. The whole area began to shake. Water swished from side to side. Sammy and Sean were pummeled by sharp sea shells and small, smooth rocks. Strands of seaweed began to wrap around their legs, making it difficult to walk. Sammy pulled off the sticky green strands and quickly scrambled toward Sean, grabbing and holding him tight. His little brother started to wail. Whatever chamber they were in seemed to be swinging, first high to the right then down low and up again high to the left. The motion was making both of them nauseous. The lack of sight made them more susceptible to feeling movement. Then, the motion abruptly stopped. The water sloshed from side to side and then slowly settled down. More water was puddling on the right side, which made Sammy think they were situated on the side of a hill.

Unexpectedly, Sean and Sammy began tumbling around and around. Their environment spinning and turning upside down. The force of the water and sand poured from the bottom to the top, separating them. They could hear each other gurgling and gasping for air as they somersaulted in circles.

Just as abruptly as it started, the chaos stopped. They poked their heads out of the watery sandy mound. The brothers grabbed each other in delight, wrapping their five sets of legs around each other and squeezing tight. Their rounded exoskeletons clicked like castanets as they rolled back and forth in joy. Their feathery antennae intertwined. Their club-shaped eye stalks simultaneously rotated 360 degrees, first in one direction and then the other, happily scanning the familiar scene. They were back home. On the beach. They saw their mother frantically scurrying toward them. They both skittered backward to reach her.

Sammy and Sean looked up at the sky and saw a boy towering above them, running up from the ocean's edge, wildly swinging a bright-red, plastic bucket from side to side.

Further up the beach the boy's father stood waving his arms. "C'mon, son! Hurry up! We're gonna' grab a burger at Opie's for lunch!" When his son reached him, he fondly tousled his hair while he proudly praised him. "You're a good boy for letting your two sand crabs go!"

A shadow briefly covered Sammy and Sean as they watched the boy run away. Without warning, they both felt a sharp pinch, followed by the wind as it whipped though their antennae. Their five sets of legs were pinned against their exoskeletons. They were bewildered. They looked down and saw the ocean beneath them, the waves cresting and crashing onto shore. At the exact same moment, the sand crabs felt a sharp, shooting pain as their back shells cracked wide open. The seagull raised his beak up toward the sky, opened it wide, and gulped Sammy and Sean into its gullet.

The bird swooped down and around in a circular motion, returning to scan the shoreline for more tasty morsels—the day was young and full of promise.

SLAY TIME

Girls and boys come out to slay.
The moon doth shine as bright as day.
Bring an axe or bring a knife.
Here to claim another's life.
Come with one blade, come with two.
Stick it in all the way through.
Up the ladder! Then push them off.
Laugh until you choke and cough.
You draw blood and I'll draw guts.
Then cook their flesh
with roasted nuts.

PETER, THE PUMPKIN EATER

Peter Peter,
pumpkin eater.
Had a wife and
tried to beat her.
She stuffed him in a pumpkin shell.
Then she baked him very well.

US 120 NORTH

David W. Dutton

THE SNOW WAS FALLING MUCH faster than before. It began twelve hours ago, and had since become a driving blizzard. Since leaving Augusta early that morning, we hadn't encountered any other vehicles on the desolate stretch of highway known as US 120 North. We were alone but for the green pines, the snow, and the winding strip of asphalt that was rapidly becoming obliterated. The last sign had placed Jackman Station one-hundred odd miles ahead.

This fool's journey had begun early the previous day after a phone call from Uncle Julius the night before. Aunt Louise was dying, and she wanted to see us. Of course, nothing would do except for us to leave as soon as possible. As a result, I had been dragged from our warm apartment in Boston and started on this lonely road to Quebec City.

My wife, Marge, and her mother were asleep in the back seat of the big BMW, and my brother-in-law, Ralph, was staring moodily out the window at the never-changing landscape of trees and snow. Through the snow-clogged windscreen, a sign was barely discernible: Jackman Station 89. If we could make it there, the worst would be behind us. It was simply this isolated stretch of highway that was so daunting.

Ralph turned from the window and stretched his arms in front of him.

"This whole thing is ridiculous! We haven't seen or heard from Aunt Louise and Uncle Julius, except for a Christmas card each year, since you and Marge were married. Why is it so important that we go see them now?"

I smiled. "Well, he *is* your mother's brother. Maybe she's feeling guilty."

Ralph laughed. "Guilty? Mother? Mother has never felt guilty in her life."

I had to agree. Rachel Robertson was one of the most self-centered women I had ever known. Certainly, there had to be some other motivation.

The road was getting worse. I only hoped that we could get to Jackman Station before the snow got too deep. The big BMW was a tank, but there was only so much that it could handle.

An hour passed, and with each minute of that hour, I had to slow the car's speed in order to stay on the road. The snow continued to fall, and by the end of the hour had drifted completely across the road. Ralph was asleep by then, but Marge had finally awakened.

Yawning and stretching, Marge moved to the edge of the seat and placed her hand on my shoulder.

"Tired?"

"A little."

"How much longer?"

"About sixty miles to Jackman."

"Road bad?"

"Pretty slippery. Snow tires don't help much once they're clogged with snow. I wish . . ."

At that moment I missed the curve. Even at such a slow speed, I was unable to stop. As Marge screamed, the car spun out of control and slid off the road and down a small embankment. When it came to rest, everyone was awake. Marge was crying.

I quickly released my safety belt and turned in my seat.

"Are you hurt?"

Marge shook her head. "No, just shaken up."

"Mother?"

"I'm fine. What a mess!" Mrs. Robertson smoothed her hair and tried to look out the window. "Poor Louise. We're never going to make it to Quebec in time."

8

Opening his door with a shove, Ralph stepped out into the snow.

"Mother, I think I'd worry about getting out of here before I thought any more about getting to Quebec."

Joining Ralph outside the car, I surveyed the damage. The hood had disappeared into a deep drift, and the whole car seemed to be buried up to its chassis. It was beyond any help we could administer. Ralph pulled out his cell phone and punched at its screen.

"Nothing. No bars at all." He stuck his head back into the car. "Either of you have signal?"

A brief pause was followed by negative responses. He looked at me and shrugged.

"What do you think, Rob?"

"The heat's only going to last as long as the gas does. Our chances of anyone coming along seem pretty slim."

"So we walk." Ralph leaned back into the car. "Come on. We're going to have to walk."

We all knew that the chances of finding any form of civilization were slight, but no one said anything. Even Mrs. Robertson didn't complain. Anything was better than just sitting there. While Ralph held the door, I helped the women out of the car. Luckily, they wore tall boots, but Ralph and I wore only street shoes. It wasn't going to be easy.

Ralph motioned to the encroaching forest of pines.

"If we stay within the tree line and follow the road that way, it shouldn't be as bad."

Leaving the car, we sought the shelter of the trees. For over an hour, we plodded along, seeing nothing but snow and trees. We stopped only when absolutely necessary.

Pausing to catch my breath, I glanced at my watch which read 1:30 PM. Thirty minutes later we saw a sign that held hope. It advertised an inn three miles ahead on our left. But it was a long three miles. The snow was blinding and cold, so blinding that we didn't see the road until we came to a sign on the other side of it.

No one said anything about the likelihood of its being vacant or long since destroyed. We simply helped one another along and kept silent. At times, on that last stretch, I didn't think we'd make it. I did all I could to help Marge, and Ralph was busy helping his mother.

Finally, the snow began to abate. It didn't stop entirely, but enough for us to see where we were going. We reached the edge of the tree line and stepped into a large clearing. Ahead of us was a large hill with a few pines scattered on and around it. At the top of the hill was the inn.

The inn was as desolate looking as its surrounding. It was huge, ugly, and Victorian in every sense of the word. The walk up the hill was long, but no one complained. We were just happy to have found a place of refuge.

We crossed the wide, snow-swept porch to the massive front door. I lifted the heavy gargoyle knocker and let it fall back into place. No one came. Perhaps it was unoccupied. I knocked again. After the third time, a woman's voice from behind the door called out.

"Who is it?"

For a second, I hesitated. "Customers. We've had some trouble with our car, and we . . ."

Slowly the door opened, admitting us to the vastness of the inn. Marge and I followed Ralph and Mrs. Robertson into the inn's lobby. The interior was like the rest of the building—Victorian. The big French doors lacked drapes or shutters, allowing the grayness of snow and sky to blend with the shadows of the room.

From behind the door, a short, wrinkled woman came forward. Her hair was neatly coiled, and the pair of pince-nez perched on the end of her nose made one notice her quiet elegance rather than her overall appearance.

"I'm afraid we are closed for the winter." Her accent was heavily English.

I looked at Ralph and then back to the lady in front of me.

"We don't expect hotel service. Our car went off the road a few miles from here. We were hoping you could put us up until the snow stopped, and we're able to call someone to dig out car out."

The woman straightened her glasses. "That's going to be somewhat difficult. The lines are down."

"Oh, please! We couldn't bear going out in that snow again!" Mrs. Robertson looked pleadingly at the proprietress. "We'll gladly pay you whatever you ask."

"I'm afraid you have not given me much choice. You will,

however, have to eat what we eat."

Marge smiled and brightened at the prospect. "That's quite all right. We wouldn't want to put you to any trouble. All we want is a place to stay until the storm ends."

I stepped forward. "Thank you so much. I'm Rob Hancock. This is my wife, Marge, and this is my mother-in-law, Rachel Robertson and her son, Ralph. We're from Boston on our way to Quebec."

The elderly woman nodded and smiled stiffly. "How many rooms will you require?"

I returned the smile. "Three, if it's not too much trouble."

"Let me see what I can do." With this, she turned and disappeared up the heavy, walnut staircase.

Not much later, a tall rail of a man came down the stairs.

"The Missus has your rooms ready. If you will follow me."

We followed him up the wide stair to the first floor of rooms where he showed Marge and me the room we would occupy. It was dark with heavy Victorian furniture and a musty odor.

"The Missus will have tea waiting for you in the lounge once you are settled."

He then left to escort the others to their rooms. Mrs. Robertson waved coyly as they left. At least she wasn't complaining.

The lounge was a big room filled with many sofas, chairs, and tables. A fire burned brightly in the marble fireplace. Marge crossed the room to stand in front of it, warming her hands.

"This feels great."

Tea was set out on a long, marble-topped side table: two tea pots, cups, saucers and serving plates of fine china, as well as biscuits and pastries. I poured a cup of steaming tea and looked over my shoulder at Marge.

"Tea, dear?"

"In a minute. I'm enjoying this fire."

I crossed the room and sat on one of the sofas facing the fireplace. Taking a sip of my tea, I picked up a copy of the *Boston Globe*, which lay on the coffee table in front of me. The bold-face type of the headline glared at me:

Titanic Sinks, Astor and Straus Among the Dead

I stared for a moment. The date was clearly 1912, but the newspaper showed very little sign of wear. I assumed it to be a novelty reproduction—the type that depict historic events. I'd seen them advertised in gift catalogs.

The newspaper was distributed on April 15, the day following that disastrous event. Below the headline was a photo of the ill-fated vessel, though it was actually that of her sister ship, the *Olympic*. The lack of a forward-enclosed promenade testified to that fact. The bulk of the article was sketchy, much of it incorrect.

I looked up as Ralph and Mrs. Robertson entered the room. Ralph crossed immediately to the tea table, and Mrs. Robertson joined Marge in front of the fire.

"Well, you must see where they have put me. On the third floor, mind you. I don't see why we couldn't be within hailing distance of one another. It's not as if the place is crowded."

Ralph joined me on the sofa, his tea sloshing over its rim and into its saucer.

"I know what you mean. I'm in the back wing on the second floor. Of course, I prefer it to the car right now."

Marge laughed.

"Yes, I wouldn't say we were in any position to complain."

Ralph poured the overflow from his saucer into his cup. He then set the cup on the newspaper to soak up the excess spillage.

"Careful, old man." I reached for the cup, but was too late. The newspaper had absorbed the tea, leaving a definite circle where it had sat. "That's one of those collector newspapers."

"Oops, sorry." Ralph folded the newspaper in half, hiding the stain.

"There. No one's the wiser. I'll send them a new one when we get home."

"Sure you will."

Marge and Mrs. Robertson busied themselves at the tea table. Mrs. Robertson finished first and took one of the chairs next to the fireplace.

"Speaking of home, when do you think we'll get out of here?"

"Hard to say," I sighed. "Hopefully there's someone nearby who can give us a hand with the car."

Mrs. Robertson sipped her tea.

"Well, I certainly hope so. When I think of poor Louise up

there alone in Quebec . . ."

"Mother, she's hardly alone. She has Uncle Julius."

Ralph cut his eyes in my direction.

"Well, you know what I mean."

"Yes, Mother, I know what you mean."

Dusk came and with it came more snow. None of us strayed far from the fireplace. It was warmer there than anywhere else in the inn. The building seemed susceptible to the wind, which piled snow under the porch rail and window sills.

Dinner was announced at 7:00 PM. The meal wasn't a gay affair. No one said anything, and the food was not terribly good. After dinner, the four of us gathered around a table to play bridge until the tall case clock in the corner chimed ten. After one final hand, we boxed the cards and climbed the stairs to the upper regions of the drafty building.

I fell asleep almost instantly and didn't remember a thing until the pounding upon the door began. Rising out of bed, I stumbled across the semi-dark room and opened the door as far as the chain would allow. It was Ralph.

By the time I had undone the chain and let him into the room, Marge was awake and sitting up in bed.

"What is it, old man? You look as if you didn't sleep very well. Is anything wrong?"

Ralph looked at his sister and then sat on the edge of the bed near her. He seemed dumbfounded and disoriented.

"I can't find Mother."

Marge gasped. "What do you mean?"

"I can't find her or those two who run this place. I can't find anyone."

I was confused.

"Are you sure? This is a mighty big place."

"I got up at eight and went downstairs, but I couldn't find anyone. Then I decided to see if Mother was awake, and I couldn't find her."

Ralph's voice had taken on a note of desperation.

"She has to be here somewhere." I pulled on my trousers and a sweater and walked to the door. "Come on, Ralph. Let's take a look."

Ralph glanced at me and then at his sister.

"That's not all."

Marge laid her hand on Ralph's shoulder. "What is it?"

Ralph rose from the bed and sighed. "You'll see."

He followed me into the shadowy corridor. Marge jumped from the bed and quickly pulled on her clothes.

"Wait for me. I'm coming too."

We climbed the stairs to the third floor of rooms. We reached the room that Ralph said was his mother's, but found it empty but for one window shade that hung crookedly from its brackets. No furniture. Nothing to indicate that Mrs. Robertson had ever been there. As we stared at those four bare walls, Marge's grip on my arm relaxed suddenly. I caught her just before she hit the floor. Taking Marge in my arms, I carried her to our room and laid her gently on the bed.

The rest of the day was devoted to searching that dreadful place, but we found nothing. When Ralph and I finished, we sat before the cold fireplace and sipped some brandy that replaced the tea from the previous day.

At 6:00 PM, a somewhat-rested Marge joined us. Everything was covered with a mournful silence until the stillness was shattered by the call to supper.

The three of us ran through the ornate archway to the dining room. As we entered, the proprietress looked up from setting the table and smiled.

"Good evening."

For an instant, I was speechless.

"Where have you been?"

"We've been right here. There are very few places one can go in this weather."

"Have you seen my mother?" Marge asked, her voice on the edge of hysteria. "We can't find her anywhere."

For a moment, the woman looked perplexed. Then she smiled again.

"I hope you're hungry, but where is the other lady? Never mind. I'll call her."

Before any of us could react, she left the room. In the silence of the inn, the only sound was that of her footsteps on the stairs.

When I finally ran after her, she was nowhere to be found. We searched everywhere for her, but she was gone. We could do no more.

Ralph died that night. I guess he died because he wasn't found, but then, neither was his body. We had been asleep for several hours when we heard his screams. Marge and I rushed up the stairs to the second floor. When we reached Ralph's door, or what was supposed to be his door, we stopped. Confronting us was a solidly plastered and papered wall. From behind it, came the most terrifying screams I'd ever heard. I held Marge close to me until the screams subsided nearly five minutes later. Marge was crying. I led her back to our room. There was nothing else we could do.

The next morning, I donned my coat and stepped out in the cold. The snow had finally stopped, and the sky was clear. From the top of the hill, I could see the forest below and the highway beyond. Walking around the house, I finally located the place where Ralph's room should have been. It had been the second room above the kitchen in the rear wing. The room above the kitchen was there, but above it, there was nothing but a sloping, snow-covered roof. There was nothing to explain it, nothing to explain any of what had happened.

I reentered the inn and walked to the foot of the wide stairway.

"Marge! You coming down?"

There was a moment of silence. Then her voice floated down the staircase.

"Be right down. Did you find anything?"

"Nothing. I'll tell you about it when you come down."

I removed my coat and laid it across a chair. What in hell was going on? I stared thoughtfully at the snow-covered landscape.

Several minutes passed before I realized that Marge hadn't appeared. I walked to the foot of the stair and laid one hand on the ornate newel post. "Marge! Marge, are you coming down?"

The silence of the lobby was the only reply.

"Marge!"

Again, there was no reply. Where was she? I climbed the stairs two at a time and entered our room. It was empty. Marge was gone. Just like Ralph and Mrs. Robertson, Marge was gone.

Gripped with panic, I ran down the stairs, grabbed my coat and struggled into it.

Outside, the sun was blinding as it reflected on the snow. Leaving the porch, I stumbled and fell on my way down the hill.

I was desperate. First, it had been Mrs. Robertson, then Ralph, then Marge. I'd be next. By the time I reached the base of the hill, I was exhausted, but I couldn't stop. Gaining my footing, I struggled along the tree-shaded road until I reached the highway. I could go no further. The last thing I remembered was hailing an oncoming SUV before I fainted.

I awoke, lying on a bed in what appeared to be a motel room. The walls were covered in knotty pine. Hunting-plaid curtains hung at the window, and several cheap wildlife prints adorned the walls. Marge sat on the edge of the bed beside me.

"Marge! How did you get here? You're all right! Where were you?"

Marge seemed uncertain at first, but then she smiled.

"Just be quiet, dear. We're all fine. The doctor says you'll be able to travel tomorrow morning."

"The doctor? Where am I?"

"Jackman Station. You'd been gone about three hours when an SUV came along and picked us up. We found you up the road where you'd passed out. We were all lucky he came along when he did."

My mind was in turmoil.

"Everyone's here?"

"Yes. Everyone's fine. They've sent a wrecker after the car. We'll be able to get to Quebec tomorrow, but there's no rush. Mother called Uncle Julius this morning. Aunt Louise is much improved. We can take our time getting there."

Three hours. It had seemed like three days. And the inn? What about the inn? Was it all a hallucination? Some kind of a nightmare?

"Are you hungry? I told Mother and Ralph we would meet them at the café for lunch," Marge smiled. "That is, if you feel like it."

I took her hand and squeezed it. "I'm starved."

Lunch was a jovial affair. Everyone seemed happy to be together. I did my best to follow their lead, but my memories of the inn fought to crowd out everything else. Obviously, it had never happened, but why did I remember it so clearly?

As we left the cafe, Marge grabbed my hand.

"There's this cute antiques shop next door. Since we have the rest of the day, I'd like to see what they have."

Everyone was in agreement and filed into the cluttered shop. It offered a wide variety of items, from furniture to books to crystal to jewelry. In a matter of minutes, we had each gone our separate ways in search of some unneeded treasure.

As I was looking at a showcase containing a wide selection of scrimshaw, Ralph came up behind me and laid his hand on my shoulder.

"Hey, Rob, there's something you need to see."

I smiled. "Sure. Lead on."

I followed Ralph through a warren of display cases and bookshelves until we arrived at the rear wall of the shop. The wall was covered in rough barn board and was used to display a variety of artwork.

"What do you think of that?" Ralph pointed to a large framed piece in the center of the display.

I stared at the front page of a newspaper that shouted the headline:

Titanic Sinks, Astor and Straus Among the Dead

"Neat, huh?"

I nodded dumbly. It wasn't the yellowed newspaper that disturbed me. It was the round stain of a tea cup marring the newsprint that sent a creeping cold down my spine.

JACK SPLAT

Jack Splat boiled the boy Matt.
His wife most enjoyed his spleen.
And so, between them both, you see,
Another corpse was clean.

DUMPTY HUMPTY

Dumpty Humpty sat on a wall.
Dumpty Humpty hit by a gull.
Then the birds gathered.
And all the fowl ate.
Hens regurgitated Humpty
for chicks to partake.

DEFUNCTS' DAY

Dianne Pearce

ANNALIE PERCH HAD BEEN A part-time professor now for 20 years. "Adjunct" was the dreadful word typically used to describe Annalie's occupation:

ad·junct ˈaˌjəNGkt/ *noun*: a thing added to something else as a supplementary rather than an essential part.

An unessential part, well, no one could say it was a career choice, but it paid the bills in a barely sort of way, and kept Annalie from one of her least favorite things to do–being stuck at a random desk in a random office for 40 hours per week, where even peeing or eating were done on a measure-tight schedule because the main thing the desk surfer was paid for was keeping his or her butt attached to the seat for as long as possible. The seat, paradoxically, usually had wheels attached, as if to further taunt the occupant with the forbidden mobility. So, though the title offensive, the pay low, the work take-home, and the hours odd, Annalie had yet to figure out another way to pay the bills and keep free, able to move. When she stepped outside after an hour or two at the podium (where she pretended she knew what she was doing), she was on her own until her next gig. She hopped into her car, and motored, maybe to coffee, maybe to her favorite plant store, maybe to the next podium, maybe to her bed, but she was free, and at any time she could make a wrong turn, on accident or on purpose, and get lost, and escape, and no one could stop her; there was no boss in the office by the door to ask for one last thing, or to note when she came and went. For all of these things, Annalie was very grateful.

And perhaps it was that gratitude that kept her late after class, pretty much every class. There was usually a line of students wanting to ask her questions, and Annalie never knew if it was because she was sort-of faking it, so in her teaching style she was a bit vague and dreamy, making some students need clarification, or if it was because they just wanted one teacher who knew them, knew their faces and their names, and cared if they showed up. Whatever their reasons, Annalie was happy to be there for them, and *with them*, clarifying, empathizing, hanging-out.

Tonight it was almost 11:30 when the last girl left. She was one of the many K girls—Kierstyn, Kailyn, Kristy, Keegan—Annalie was pretty sure this one had been Kiley, telling Annalie her tearful story of having been diagnosed with ADHD, and Annalie had spent no little time trying to prove to her that she, Kiley, or was it Kirsty, was not her diagnosis. "You're going to do just fine, and I know, because you're already doing fine, here, now. You're a very good student." Annalie had a lot of affection and sympathy to give her, hugs had been exchanged a few times, so the time got away from them both, making it very late when little Kleenex finally wiped her face with Annalie's tissues and went home.

Then Annalie had to pack up herself and get out the door. Tonight she had been teaching in the distance ed. room, so she had to shut down the system that broadcast her to the other two students at the remote campus: the phone, the many screens around the room, the cameras, and the sound system. As usual she did this all, and began then to erase the boards and pack up her own things. And as usual in this large, old, musty, sound-proofed room, the damn system phone started ringing. There was a glitch in the coordination on the other end, so even though Annalie turned everything off, the other system, 80 miles away, turned it back on, and tried to start up again. Next the room fan would respond and come back on, and the doors to the room—double doors in the far right corner, heavy, wooden, and swing-mounted, like church doors—started swooshing back and forth about two inches against each other and the frame. Each time this happened, and tonight was no different, Annalie jumped about a foot. Yep, heart was still working. Good to know for a person without health insurance. That was her standard joke. Then she would run over to the command central and push the "hang-up" button, and the whole works would shut down again, and the overhead lights would re-dim to walking lights only.

"Christ, what a pain in the ass," she said as she walked back to the last board she had been erasing.

She heard a whirr sort-of sound above her head, and her neck snapped back. One of the cameras above her was moving, searching for a person to focus on.

"Fuck!" she said, and ran back to the command station desk.

She quickly pushed all the shut-down buttons again, before the phone could start ringing, and then ran over to her bag, slammed the lid on her laptop, yanked its cord from the wall, and started shoving it into her bag. The doors did a whoosh again. Annalie froze, and stared at them in the dim walk light, looking for a shadow or form of a person. There was none. In the opposite corner from the door was the command desk. Annalie's eyes shot left; no one was there. She jammed her cord into her bag without really looking at it, and started shoving books in on top, telling herself to calm down and hurry up at the same time. There was a whir. She stopped. She waited. She peeked under her brow, up at the ceiling. Whirrr! All six little cameras started spinning like mad in their little trapezes, searching for a person.

"Fuck!" Annalie said.

She shoved her chalk into the bag on top of the books, grabbed her little pack of tissues and her sweater from the chair, and ran for the door. Just as she went out the double doors of the room the phone started ringing, but this time through the speakers, loud. She looked up and down the dim halls. The building was empty. Her heart was pounding. She could see her car outside, under one of the light poles in the parking lot. It was alone.

"Maintenance or the cleaning man can deal with it tomorrow," she said, sprinting toward the glass door to the lot.

She reached her car. There was no one behind her. Unlike the doors to the room, the double doors to the building had opened because she had hurled herself into the panic bar, and closed behind her swiftly and with an audible click. She was safe. She pushed the lock button on the ignition key and the hatch popped open. She threw her bag in and slammed the hatch. She ran to the driver's door, flung it open, and threw in her purse. She grabbed the lever to flip the seat forward, and scanned the back seat for any psychos hiding there. She saw no one. She flipped the seat back and fell on to it; she slammed the door against herself and hit the lock button on the arm. She put her key in the ignition, turned it, and put on her high beams. There was no one in front of the car. She put on the interior lights and twisted around, checking again for psychos in the back, or the hatch; there was no one.

She buckled in and pulled from her spot and out of the little faculty lot, then she turned and went back in. She headed for the distance ed. building. She sat there, with her high beams boring into the glass doors of the building, about twenty-five feet away across the grass between the lot's concrete frame and the walk to the doors. Inside she saw . . . nothing. No movement, no figures in the dark, no glitter of eyes looking back at her. The broadcasting room was soundproofed, and so had no windows or access to the outside. If it was going flaming bonkers mad in there, she couldn't tell. "God bless the janitor!" she said, and slowly turned her car around, and left the lot again, winding her way through campus to the exit. When her wheels hit the road it was just midnight, November 2.

The whole world was black whenever she left this campus at night. Because it was in rural Maryland, Annalie always made sure she had a full tank of gas before she went to school; the nearest station was twenty-three miles away. The nearest town was farther, and both were off the main road, which was itself a mere two-lane affair with a grassy median that was usually littered with carcasses of deer, coons, and cats. Luckily, at night, she couldn't see the dead things. She couldn't see anything, really, except to tell if the corn in a particular field was still there or not. The corn farmers let the corn dry out before they harvested, so it either stood in the fields like dead saplings, or, after cutting, left little dried stumps like stubble across the ground, giving it a post-apocalyptic look in either sense. Because corn was so light colored, it reflected the high beams while the rest of the landscape just soaked the light in, like raw wood soaking up paint.

The GPS said it was one hour and forty-five minutes to home, said it was forty-seven degrees, and painted a little purple line to lead her to her bed. Annalie turned on NPR, as usual. She lucked-out on an interesting interview show. John Hockenberry was inter-viewing an author who'd just published a compendium of religious holidays.

"And so tomorrow is All Souls Day, as you said, but you put in here that it is also called Defuncts' Day?"

"Indeed. That was the name given to it by Pope Stephen the VI, and by all accounts it had to do with him digging up his predeces-sor and putting the corpse on trial."

"Well, how do you mean?"

"He, Stephen, decided that the dead who had died while out of favor with the Papacy, or God in general, would not even be given the dubious blessing of going to Purgatory to work through their sins; no, rather they would become 'defuncts,' because, dying without giving proper due to The Lord, they were no longer relevant to God, so why would God waste effort torturing them in Purgatory when they were really not-functioning souls according to His doctrine?"

"In other words, Stephen thought that Purgatory was a pun-ishment, but one the wicked had to earn?"

"Undeniably John. To be sure, he was not a nice man, nor a very beloved Pope."

"Wow, so, was there no recourse for sinners during his reign?"

"Well, Stephen enjoyed money, as much as he did power, and people could buy indulgences for the lost, just as had always been the way in the church."

"So the poor people became the majority of the defuncts?"

Annalie's eyes stared wearily at the glowing lines on the edges of the black road, flicking up to check the purple trail on the GPS. Hockenberry's voice was so soothing. She might have to switch to the rock station.

"Well, you'd think so, but one could always trade a person for an indulgence."

"You mean give a son to the priesthood?"

"No, I mean donate yourself, or your wife, or your child, give a person, in the literal sense, to the Pope."

"What would the Pope do with a person?"

"Enslave him or her perhaps, maybe prey on the sacrifice sexually, maybe take out his frustrations in torture, maybe simply sacrifice the person, give the blood to The Lord."

"Really?"

"Oh my God!" said Annalie, "the freaking crazy Catholics!"

"Oh John," said the speaker, "we weren't that far from paganism at this point, and let's not forget this was not limited to popes. If one reads my book, we have hundreds of religious observances all over the world, from China to Quebec, that involve some form of human sacrifice to redeem a family member who has died out of favor with the tenants of the time. It's usually, of course, been daughters who were sacrificed, or a very young son, people known to be kind hearted, those willing to take on others' pain."

"That's fascinating, and so…"

"OMG, I am falling asleep John!" yelled Annalie. She reached for and twirled the dial, but found nothing but static. She tried to find her way back to the NPR station, but that, too, seemed to be gone. "Shit! How long have I been in this fucking car?" She looked ahead at the road while turning down the volume on the static where John Hockenberry had been. She could see lights ahead. That was good. Lights meant she was coming into Ellendale, and close to home. The light grew closer. Annalie switched off the cruise control and let the car slow down, because all the little towns in Delaware had speed limits of twenty-five. It was odd, though; this looked to be a fair amount of lights ahead. Ellendale usually had only the light from the fire department, and the sign from the Southern Grille. Annalie kept squinting. It was a lot of lights. Her eyes darted back to the GPS. Still on the purple line. It said she had, still ninety minutes? To get home? That couldn't be right if this was Ellendale. The lights were collecting the fog around them, taking them out of focus, but then, like a snap of your fingers, she could tell what she was looking at. That wasn't Ellendale ahead.

It was the goddamn school!

Annalie couldn't believe it. She pulled up until she was parallel with the entrance and stopped. She didn't even bother to pull to the side; unless some farmer had a heart attack there would not be anyone on this road. Yep, the school. Crazy. It must have been Hockenberry's fault. She must have taken a wrong turn, hit the wrong button on the GPS.

She reached for the cord that charged her cell phone to call her husband and whine. He was likely asleep already. She reeled the cord in. There was no phone on it. Annalie panicked. She jumped out of the car, ran around to the other side, flung open the door, searched her purse, her bag, pulled the laptop out roughly, spilling the books and chalk onto the road. No phone in there. She threw the detritus back in, and gave herself a full-body pat-down. No phone. She slammed the passenger door and ran back to the other side, got on her knees in the road in the night, and looked and felt under her seat, no phone. She laid her head on the seat for a second, and, whoosh, there was the sensation of a car screaming past her fast enough to rock her little hatchback. She screamed, and leapt up, but there was no car to be seen anywhere; the landscape was as still and black as the college was still and bright. She decided that she better get out of the road and into the light. She got back in and drove into the parking lot.

She knew, damn it, that the cell phone must be in her classroom. The only thing was, those doors went on lockdown after a certain time, which is why they had the panic bars to allow late students and teachers to leave. She drove around the whole campus looking for a maintenance or security person. No one seemed to be on the campus. She went to the security booth, no one was there. She went to the main building; it was so dark she didn't even bother getting out of her car. So, well, she was pretty certain between cleaners and students her cell would not be there in the morning, and it had been a big splurge, the latest iPhone, so that she could check student emails on the road. She was still paying on it. She drove slowly back around the full length of the one-way only campus, and into the little parking lot of the distance ed. building. She parked her car and sat there, gathering courage.

The building looked dark and quiet. It was just a short walk across the grass from where she was in the handicapped spot(even in this dead campus at 1:00 AM she had guilt about parking in a handicapped spot, but she wanted to be as close as she could be to escape!). She switched off the headlights, because even though she saw no one here, she did not want to attract attention. She inhaled deeply, as if taking a dive off a high dive, and stepped out of her car, pushed the door softly closed, and pushed the lock button on the key, twice, so that she would not have to check for psychos again when she got back.

She ran lightly and quietly across the grass to the doors, a cat-burglar now. She hit the cement, and pushed against the doors. Solid. Oh, wait. She pulled the handle of one, hard; it opened with ease, sending her on to her butt on the cement. She lost her grip as she fell, but she bounced up like a Bozo punching bag and grabbed the handle just before it clicked back into place. Lucky, it must not have closed tightly when she left before, and she was so glad of this that she stepped in and headed for the classroom as breezily as if it was only the afternoon.

Usually, in the schools, when you walked into a dark hall or classroom, the lights came on by motion. They did not do that though, which Annalie noticed when she stuck her toe into the carpet and tripped herself, halfway to the classroom. She caught herself and paused. She waved her hands in the air like she was on a desert island signaling a plane. The plane did not see her. The sensors did not see her. She stopped waving, nervously checked the dark hall out before and behind her, and slowly, tiptoeing now, went on.

The classroom was quiet, when she pushed open the doors. There were no moving cameras, no fans, no ringing phones, some of the chairs had been neatened, and she wondered if maintenance had been in. Yes, in the safety lights of the classroom she could see her phone, on the ledge of the chalkboard, a circle drawn around it in chalk. "That was so nice of them not to steal it, and not to make me go to lost and found!" she thought. She felt fine now, and she walked forward with confidence and picked up her phone. It looked fine, and as she turned back toward the door, she pressed the home button to see if she could call Greg.

Her finger depressed the button, but instead of the phone coming on, the full lights of the room came on, the cameras whirred and spun, the phone started ringing, the fans came on, high, and the heavy doors whooshed back and forth as if a gunslinger had just walked through. Annalie screamed and dropped her phone. Everything stopped. The room went back to the dim safety lights. She squinted in the darkness, shaking and covered in goosebumps, frozen in her spot. She squinted and squinted. Then she breathed. Then she moved a little. The swinging doors had come to a stop. She twisted her head around. The room was still empty. "Oh my God it's possessed in here," she said aloud. She bent down wearily and picked up her phone. "What a story this will be," she said as she leaned back up. The back wall met her eyes. It appeared to have motion.

"It is, most certainly, possessed in here," a voice said.

Annalie screamed again. The safety lights slowly got a little brighter. In the back of the room she could see, now, the six students who usually sat in the front row of her class. They were assembled in a loose triangle with her favorite student, Patrick, in the front. His red hair glinted in the bright uplight, and it was he who had spoken.

"Patrick? Joe? Krenna? Deshawn? Keegan? Kerrianna? What? Why aren't you guys home? You left a long time ago. Oh my God, am I dreaming?" Annalie did what she had always done when she found herself trapped in a nightmare, she shut her eyes tight and screamed, loud and hard and long. She didn't wake up, no one woke her up, and when she opened her eyes she could see that the K-girls looked at her with concern.

"Patrick are you sure this is going to work?" said Keegan.

"Yes," said Patrick, his hands clasped in front of him. "I know. I've taken two of her classes. I know how she is."

"Patrick?" she asked, trying to sound as teacherie as possible. "What—"

"Mrs. Perch," he said, "you're not dreaming. We are here. We are here because of you. You're so great Mrs. Perch. All your students love you."

Annalie looked at them. They were nice students, even the K-girls. She felt embarrassed for screaming. She wondered if she was somehow confused about the time. She was teaching a lot of extra classes this semester, trying to pay off some debt, like the one for the phone in her hand, and she was mentally fried. "Wait, you guys, am I messed up on the time?" The time glowed from her phone suddenly. Its light startled her and she almost dropped it again, as if it was hot to touch, but she caught it reflexively with her left hand. It clearly said 1:30 AM. "Oh my God!" she gasped, "am I dead?" She thought of the car she'd felt whoosh past her on the road. She backed up into the chalkboard.

"Oh, Mrs. Perch, no," said Patrick, leaning forward and smiling a slightly weird, slightly sour smile. "Ha ha, oh no, you know, you're not dead or anything."

"Ha ha, oh no, no," the other students echoed in a hollow chorus.

"But we are," said Patrick, snapping upright again, his eyes narrowing into slits that glowed orange like his locks, "and we don't like it at all, you see."

His voice rang with bitterness; it was so sour Annalie could almost taste it. It chilled her to her bones. She put her right hand behind her and grasped the chalkboard ledge. Her face flushed. She squeezed her eyes tight and turned her cheek against the cold slate. She waited for her lungs to stop constricting. She listened. There was no sound. Her phone made the text noise she had chosen, the honk of a clown horn. She opened her eyes without thinking and looked at the phone.

GREG "Fell asleep on sofa. Just woke up & UR not 🏠. RUOK?"

It normalized everything. She was going to be okay. She looked around the room. It had returned to its usual quiet, dim state.

She pushed the voice button and dictated, "Oh, fuck me, yes. Left my stupid phone in class, and had to come back. Am so tired I hallucinated or something. Phew. Need sleep. Leaving now. Can we call out tomorrow?"

GREG "I can, sure."

"OK. Call me then, and talk to me until I get out of here and am home?"

GREG "Sure."

"Call right now."

GREG "Dialing."

The phone rang. Annalie gave a big sigh and started walking toward the door and then hit the accept button and the speaker button.

"Greg, can you hear me?"

"Hi Mrs. Perch."

"Greg?" She stopped walking, looked at the phone. The name above the control panel said GREG.

"Hi Mrs. Perch. This is Patrick, from class."

"Greg, what the fuck, that is not funny!"

"No, no, it's not funny, and it's not Greg. I had no idea, even after two classes, that you cursed so much," Patrick said in his soft, spacey voice.

"What?!"

"Um, Mrs. Perch, I was hoping you'd calmed down now. We're in the back of the room still, you see?"

She looked straight at the back wall, and she did see. Patrick's hair glowed. She screamed and dropped the phone yet again. Patrick gave a short laugh and came toward her, and she backed away, into the padded side wall.

"Patrick, this is not working," said one of the K-girls.

Patrick waved at her with a fast angry swipe of his arm that moved the air in the room so much that the doors began to swing again. The K-girls backed into the darker part of the room together. "Listen Mrs. Perch," Patrick said, stooping to pick up her phone, "we really want you to hang on to your phone. We know you're teaching a lot to get this." He stopped about a foot away from her and leaned forward and gingerly, slowly, pushed it into her coat pocket. Annalie sucked in her breath. Patrick froze, and looked up at her from under his hair, his eyes blue and pale, cool and human.

"Patrick?" As his hand came slowly up from her pocket Annalie reached her hand toward it. He turned his palm up, and left his hand open for inspection in the air between them, like she was a frightened stray. She touched it with a finger, poked it, really. Then she clasped his fingers in hers. "You're real."

"Yes, sure. I'm your student. I got an A in your lit class."

"But you're so cold."

"Yes, I am; we all are." he waved toward the shadows.

"What's going on? Is this a game or something?"

"It's a request. We need some help; we need some extra help."

"Well I don't understand. You know you can have extra help anytime. I'll even stay late after class."

"We needed the other students to leave, so we needed you to go, and come back. We needed help in private."

"So we took your phone," said one of the K-girls, "and we're sorry about that."

"I put John Frankenberry on your radio," said Deshawn with a big smile. "I think he's a little boring Mrs. Perch."

"It's *Hockenberry*, Deshawn, and he's a wonderful host," Annalie replied automatically.

"*Frankenberry's* more fun, but I'm sorry."

"Wait, what exactly do you mean you put him on my radio, Deshawn?"

"Oh my God this is taking forever!" wailed one of the K-girls.

"Be patient!" Patrick snarled. "How long do you think you'll wait without her?" He turned and looked at them, and one of the K-girls' knees buckled, but Deshawn caught her as she crumpled, and lifted her back to standing. Patrick, hand still waiting in the air, moved it so that he was clasping Annalie's fingers, and drew her out a bit from the wall. "Can I have your other hand, Mrs. Perch?"

She put her hand in his, afraid to refuse him.

"Thank you. Our story, what we need to tell you, what we need help with, well, it's a bit of a story, but I'll try to be quick. It's Defuncts' Day, Mrs. Perch"

"What is that?"

"I know you heard Hockenberry in the car."

"Oh, yes."

"We're Defuncts, Mrs. Perch"

"I see. You're sinners?"

"Yes, in effect, we are. But, to be more specific, we are people The Lord simply doesn't care about."

"Oh, Patrick, I don't believe in God, all that nonsense."

"Oh, I know that, Mrs. Perch, but, unfortunately, for all of us, He is real, and He's one hell of a nasty bastard."

"What? Oh no, Patrick. I don't believe that. You're barking up the wrong teacher, honey."

Patrick turned Annalie's left hand so that the palm was face up. She yelped and pulled it away as she felt, but did not see, something scrape at it, like a cat claw.

Patrick dropped her other hand. "Look at it."

Annalie opened her hand in front of her eyes. DEFUNCT, the letters ragged and red, was scrawled into her palm. She screamed. The cameras came on above their heads and whirled uncontrollably. The speaker phone began ringing. Patrick turned and banged his hand down on the closest desk. Everything stopped. Annalie sucked in her breath.

"Ok, you don't believe, Mrs. Perch. Fine." He spoke through gritted teeth. "But He believes in you, and that is not to your favor."

Annalie said nothing, but she turned her head toward the

doors. DeShawn was there, leaning against them, and they were not swinging open from his weight as they should have. She sunk into the padded wall behind her in defeat.

"Mrs. Perch, I was raped, repeatedly, by my parish priest as a boy, and, finally, one day, he fell asleep after, and I decided I was done with him doing that to me, so I pulled my scout's knife out of my pocket and stabbed him in the neck."

She stared at him in horror.

"Yes, he didn't, well, he didn't die. But, when you're from the south . . ."

She looked at him, her head tilted, listening.

"Don't you remember, the third week of our lit class, you asked me if I was from Texas; you caught the accent."

"Oh, yes, now I remember."

"Well, in the south, they don't care too much about whether you're a child or not when you hurt an adult, so they put me in jail, the maximum security men's prison."

"Oh Patrick! I am so sorry!"

"So am I. The priest was nothing compared to the prison. I–" he took a deep breath, "Well, I didn't make it, Mrs. Perch"

"You're dead?" It came out of her throat as a gasp.

"You know I am; we told you."

"I didn't . . . I am so sorry." She looked at the other students, "Deshawn, did you have something–"

"We all had something, something horrible, something unfair, but the bastard upstairs doesn't care, our families don't care, no one cares. Mrs. Perch, they just want us to suffer, forever."

"And it's not fair and we want you to stop it!" shouted a K-girl.

"What can I do?"

"You? You can do everything. You can absorb our sins," said Patrick.

"What?"

"You can absorb our sins. You can help us escape. You can free us from this state of being forgotten, of being forever in pain. You can make it right."

"Why me?"

"Because you care about me, Mrs. Perch; I know you do."

"And me too," said DeShawn.

"And us!" said one of the K-girls.

"We love you Mrs. Perch," said another.

"And what happens to me after, after I, if I can help, will I die?" She felt herself sinking in to the padded wall.

"No, no, but if you do so, willingly, you'll get a big boost in your heaven tally; it will certainly make up for your atheism. Probably enough for you and Greg, for when, well, for when you do die."

"And what happens to you? Do you come back to life?"

"No, but we get backstage passes to the party, you see, we get to stop being used and abused; we get to be saved from Hell." He looked into her wide eyes, and nodded his head. "Oh yes, Hell is real. Nothing the priest did to me matched the prison I was sent to, and compared to Hell, prison was so, so easy."

"Prison, was easy?"

"At least in prison I was mortal. I could escape. I died. I left my body, but the afterlife is pretty physical too, and I can't escape it. Unless you give us the key."

"Oh Patrick, I just don't know that I can, that I believe. Can I think about it?"

"No, it has to be tonight. We can get out of Hell to roam the earth at night–surprise, demons are morning people–but we can only escape our fate on Defuncts' Day, and only from dusk to dawn; when those bastards clock back in, we return whether we want to or not."

"You think you don't believe, but you'll end up with us whether you believe or not," a K-girl commented.

"She doesn't care, Patrick, you were wrong!" sobbed another.

"What do I have to do?" Annalie straightened up and threw her shoulders back.

"You simply have to walk among us, let us touch you."

"Just let you touch me? What do you mean?"

Patrick took her hand again. "Just let us touch you, Dear Teacher, just walk among us, let us touch you, hold, you, and then you walk out the door and don't look back."

One of Annalie's students had once said to her. "Mrs. Perch, I bet God made you have no kids of your own on purpose, so you could love all of us like we were your kids." Was that the divine plan? Annalie could have felt used, but then she looked into Patrick's sweet, young, freckled face and saw the anguish in his eyes. "Yes, I'll help. I'll take your sin. You can all touch me."

Patrick tugged at her fingers, pulled her to him, enfolded her in his arms. "Mrs. Perch, you are the nicest teacher; I knew you cared; thank you." He kissed her cheek, he ran his fingers through her hair as though he had to have part of her entwine with him, and then he ran his hands over the length of her torso, and turned her round. She was shocked at Patrick touching her in that way, but before she could say so DeShawn was there to enfold her. He kissed her square on the mouth.

"Mrs. Perch, you are the nicest teacher; I know you care; thank you." He ran his hands over her too, fondled both her breasts, but before she could gasp out her surprise, she found herself turned again, and in the middle of the K-girls.

"Mrs. Perch, you are the nicest teacher; we know you care; thank you." They said it over and over again as their lips and hands ran over her body. There were fingers between her legs, in her ears, pulling on her hair to tilt her head back and kiss her. Annalie was thinking that this was all crazy, crazy and wrong, and so scary, when she found herself suddenly, unsteadily, released and on her feet, facing the swinging doors.

"Thank you Mrs. Perch," Patrick said, "Don't look back, just go out the door, and the next door, and when you reach your car, drive home to your life. Thank you, again!" The cameras whirred and spun, the phone came through the speaker. The lights rose and dimmed frantically, and Annalie, in a panic once again, darted forward, pushed open the doors.

The whirring light from the room hit the hall when Annalie pushed open the doors, bouncing off the old polished paneling of the walls, and lighting up the length of it.

The space looked as if every bit of it was teeming with moving, squirming, grasping life, but nothing before her eyes was alive. They were corpses, in varying stages of decay; reaching, grasping, wanting her. Annalie screamed at the sight, at the smell that gagged her, and a hand hit her square in her back, and sent her tumbling and stumbling into the crowd before her. There must have been two hundred between her and the door to fresh air and her car. She screamed again when her hands reached out to steady her, and hit rotting flesh, and the movement all around her froze. She, too, froze, and then turned and tried to return to the room she'd just left, but the swinging double doors were as unmoving as if they had a steel bar across them. She banged and banged on them. "Patrick! Patrick!" The doors were unreceptive. Her hands hurt from slamming her palms into them.

She spun around. The mass of bodies was as still as the grave, each one unmoving, each holding its breath. She looked past them to her car. She looked at them. They looked at her with what eyes they had to look with. They saw her consider the odds. They saw her begin to lurch forward. She was so white, so white and glowing in the dark. "Mrs. Perch, you are the nicest teacher; we know you care; thank you," said two-hundred voices in unison.

She screamed.

And they were upon her.

DOORKNOB JESUS

Mark Alan Polo

May the doorknob Jesus protect us from the unknown.
Anonymous Prayer

BY SUMMER OF 1974, the national gas crisis that resulted when the petroleum-producing countries proclaimed an oil embargo in October 1973, was in full bloom. Lines of cars stretched for blocks with ill tempers stretching for miles. My life strategy, while I waited in line, was to quietly come out as gay, move in with my spouse, and normalize my life as I saw it. It was all gay, all gas, all the time. Both punctuated every thought and sentence with decreased mobility and planned strategy to our every move. It figured in every thought, about our new apartment, our new business, and our new lives. In the odd-even formula for rationing gas, in which the last digit of your license plate dictated whether you could purchase fuel on an even or odd calendar day, we were relegated to odd. A fitting little irony of life as we knew it. I thus spent hours of every "odd" day in gasoline lines to get the most fuel we could buy, enabling us to advance our lives on the "even" days.

Albert had pushed for months for us to live together. One night early in August at dinner, I finally mustered up the nerve to tell my parents that I was moving out The kitchen air was humid and hot despite the oscillating fan placed behind the portable TV pulled up to the dinner table.

"So, who should I invite to my rent party for our new apartment?" I asked, as if this conversation was already in full motion. There was stunned silence as my parents cut the chuck steak in front of them.

"*Our*?" my father asked, knowing the answer.

"Yeah, Albert and I have been looking and we think we found a place we like."

My mother quietly put her fork and knife down and stood up. She walked into her bedroom just a few feet away and closed the door. A moment of silence was broken by her laudable sobs. My dad and I awkwardly sat sawing at the meat in front of us. The sobbing abruptly stopped two excruciatingly long minutes later and the bedroom door opened. Mom returned and sat down as if that blip hadn't happened. She seamlessly continued eating.

"You'll need to invite your aunts and uncles and our friends, Richie and Aggie, of course," she said. "When were you thinking of moving? We could really use your bed up in the Pennsylvania cottage."

My mother's recovery from her categories of tragedy were immediate; she'd had much practice.

"September 1," I said, without glancing up. I didn't want to read a reaction in her face. I understood her subtlety. She was a master player at life's poker game.

Turns out that the gay thing was not as big an issue for her as the moving out thing was. 1974 was an unusual time.

We found an apartment that suited us perfectly, a quirky flat owned by an even quirkier woman, Elsie, in Edgewater, New Jersey. She was about to retire from a teaching position that she'd held for forty-five years, and her need for income overrode her desire to live alone. Our friend Brandon knew Elsie for years and described her as "a harmless Ruth Gordon type."

"Ruth Gordon in *Rosemary's Baby*," Brandon winked. "But no hint of being aligned with the devil," he assured us.

Elsie lived in the flat above the apartment she was planning to rent out. A few years earlier, shortly after Elsie's husband had died, the prior tenants had abruptly vacated the dwelling. The apartment had remained vacant ever since.

Elsie met us at a huge red door of this gray turn-of-the-century house. At less than five-feet tall in flats, she stretched to look through the small glass of the door prior to unfastening the locks.

"It's Brandon, Elsie. I'm here with Albert and Mark to see the apartment." Brandon leaned into us. "She's always a little awkward with strangers at first, but she'll warm up to you quickly."

Elsie opened the door slowly and the vacuum of air rushing in fluttered the sheer curtain on the door's window. She cautiously opened the door to the apartment and let us in. We were immediately blown away upon seeing the apartment. But, at $300.00 per month, it was priced at twice our budget.

Nonetheless, we toured the weathered house, walking into a rail-road flat with vintage chestnut-trimmed windows, aged pine floors, and an antiquated bathroom and kitchen that suited us perfectly. One room followed the other. The living room lead to a dining room which lead to hallway and then the kitchen, continued through to a sun porch and a bedroom to the side. A second bedroom was located off the hall and could be repurposed as our workroom, as we were also embarking on building a partnership in interior design which we would develop while Albert sewed couture dresses to fund our wish list. We could draft, cut, and sew right there. Inspiration could flow whenever the spirit moved, day or night. With caution weakening to the wind, we signed the lease, knowing that we'd somehow manage to eke out the $300 each month.

We moved in the following week.

The move itself wasn't complicated. We had plenty of accessories and almost no furniture, so everything was packed into laundry baskets, open boxes, and bags. We piled as much as we could in the front room and when the piles increased beyond capacity, they bled into the next room. Our one large possession, a Chinese folding screen, was gently placed in the second room. It was there that we noticed a small brown spot on the floor. A second spot was soon discovered in front of a line of open boxes on the other side of the room. Albert and I stood over the spots as if having been surprised by the carcass of a dead animal. We looked at each other and then again at the spots. I tried to wipe them up but to no avail. They were greasy and smelled of urine. We assumed they were from a former pet or that a stray had somehow gotten into the long-vacant apartment.

Time passed. Bags and boxes were emptied, furniture was begged and borrowed, and we hobbled a life and a furnished apartment together. Two months in our new home we discovered that the curious spots were not only still around, but were growing. Previously the size of two donuts, the spots had expanded to pizza size, which, in turn, grew to the size of two small Volkswagens. They also grew further, spreading left to right and right to left. Month after month as we struggled to pay the rent and start our business, the freakish spots evolved. They grew so big that we covered them with large black garbage bags which we'd cut open. Before long we could actually see them expand, capturing the fibers of the wood floor like an oil spill in the gulf only in slow motion. As the stains increased, unusual activity began to manifest within the apartment. Unexplained whirling and buzzing sounds, lights flashing off and on, doors slamming of their own accord. The strangeness increased in concert with the growth of the stains.

We decided it was time to speak to Elsie. We placed cookies on a plate and climbed the stairs to her apartment. She opened the door but we were not invited inside, so we spoke at the doorway. We talked about the cookies and then segued to our problem. She physically shrank away from the conversation.

"I don't know. Why are you coming to me with this? I don't know anything."

She quietly and quickly closed the door as we stood there, cookie plate in hand. Albert and I glanced at one another then down at the cookies and shrugged our shoulders. We turned around and descended the stairs like reprimanded children. It was clear that if we intended to stay in our residence, we and we alone owned this problem.

With no support from Elsie, we went on our own hunt to unearth the reason for, and possibly identify a solution to, the cancer that was eating at our floors. We searched beneath in the sub flooring, poked and searched in the walls, looked for leaks.

Nothing.

The subflooring was bone dry. The walls showed no evidence of staining or intrusion. We looked for leaks in the foundation, checked the basement for rot or mold.

Still nothing.

With little to do but soldier on, we covered the stained floor in plastic and laid a rug over it and then hosted a dinner party for Brandon. We wanted to thank him for his help. He said he'd be bringing along five nuns that he knew from a school where he'd previously taught.

"They're a load of laughs," he said, so we cooked for five more.

The nuns were in full black regalia: white chin straps, beaded rosary belts, with additional ropes around their waists and with a large scapular hanging from each with Jesus in full metal glory. They walked in single file, smiling and laughing. The first two greeted and giggled their light introductions.

The third, Sister Agnes, walked into the flat. She stopped at the first spot on the floor, hidden under layers of plastic and broadloom. Her laughing and grinning ended and she looked as if she'd hit a wall. The fourth to enter was Sister Mary Grace, who froze as if cemented to the floor. She suddenly couldn't move.

"Help me into a chair in another room, closest to the entrance," she pleaded.

Sister Mary Grace spoke briefly with her fellow nuns.

"I'm sorry, but I need to go back to the car."

"Can we at least offer you anything?"

"We should probably leave," Sister Agnes said.

We again tried to comfort them, but to no avail. They huddled in a private conversation and emerged from their desperate prayer circle with a plan.

"We're terribly sorry about leaving so abruptly. But there is something wrong here. We hope that you'll accept our apologies for leaving so suddenly," Sister Agnes said. "But please accept a gift from us."

"Of course," I said, knowing that the cancer in the floor had become not just an inconvenient design problem but a more spiritual, supernatural event.

"Please accept these scapulars as a token from us. They will protect you." They quickly removed their crosses with Christ in tarnished gold relief and handed them to us.

"There is something wrong here and you must protect yourselves," Sister Mary Alice cautioned. "Use our scapulars. Hang them from the doorknobs and never take them down. When you move, *and you will move*, return them to us."

They left in single file, quieter, waddling and bowing their gracious goodbyes, back to their Buick. We watched as all five made the sign of the cross behind the tint of their car windows as their vehicle sped away. Albert, Brandon, and I stood at the curb, speechless.

"I'm not sure I want to go back in there," I said.

"They're just a little skittish. Don't get too upset by them," Brandon said, trying to explain the failed dinner party. "Honestly, they tend to be a bit odd at times. Never quite like this, but odd nonetheless."

Albert said nothing as he collected the crosses from us and returned to the house with a new resolve.

From that moment on, nothing was the same. After the crosses were hung from strategic doorknobs, day after day and night after night, the apartment whirled and buzzed, creaked and groaned with activity, but with an edge of anger that was previously lacking. Not only was the house alive, but it now seemed irritated by our attempt to stifle its energy. Suddenly we heard voices with a certain regularity. Once each week, a distant voice could be heard calling out to us. There existed a new level of tension in the air. It was palpable, like a scream stifled by a blanket. We considered moving out, but where would we go? Moreover, we felt powerless *to* leave, as if we were being held against our will.

Months passed and we settled into the apartment's energy. The doorknob Jesuses were our first and only line of defense. They alone helped stop the progression of the floor spots. We refinished the floors to remove the visual effects of our plight. With that our worlds blended coarsely into this place. It became our uneasy home as its oddness crept into our psyche.

Elsie remained distant. We worked hard at befriending her. The benefit was that she finally shed a bit of light on the back story.

"When my husband—when Fred—died, all the clocks in the house stopped. He laid down for a nap before dinner and he passed away. It was 5:50 PM. It was a Tuesday afternoon, while I was grading papers. All the clocks." She spoke in fragments and shook her head.

We then knew that Fred's was the voice we'd been hearing every Tuesday night while eating dinner at the kitchen table, "Help me," he begged, week after week. We originally dismissed the event, telling

40

each other that the sound was coming from outside. But we were suddenly wiser.

The voice became the cocktail party entertainment that began our evening get togethers, like camp night ghost stories with a flashlight to our chins.

More and more, the entity found inventive ways to make its presence known. Belongings would disappear, particularly anything red. Through trial and error we learned that we needed to ask for whatever had been taken away. Our request would be followed by a loud noise of something falling over in one of the rooms. Our missing item would be there, beneath whatever had fallen. Our lives twisted through these months to the point where we were not even conscious of the changes that we were going through. Lights flickered off and on during client meetings. Doors slammed shut and then reopened. We saw reflections in glass doors that didn't belong to us. Our clients took note of not only the strangeness of the events but of our lack of concern about them.

"It's just our resident ghost," Albert typically offered. "More coffee?"

Months became years. We celebrated our two-year anniversary in the apartment with having shelves built in our workroom. A good friend, Jerry, worked as a carpenter and lived in Manhattan. We bartered for services. In exchange for the shelves, we designed two outfits for his budding actress girlfriend. He was no nonsense and sweetly gruff.

"I'll spend the night. Finish up the job the next morning," Jerry suggested, upon arriving.

"You should probably know that we have, well, *entity issues* here," Albert said.

"Entity issues? You mean like ghosts and shit?"

"Yeah. Like ghosts and shit," I nodded.

"Don't worry. I can handle ghosts," Jerry said, brushing away the warning in a manner measured in high levels of testosterone. He wasted no time in starting the work, laced with a lot of male puffing, to meet whatever challenges the spirit might bring.

We went about our business while Jerry hammered and sawed. Hours into the project we heard a gasp and the halting of all noise.

Jerry walked out to the kitchen, ashen.

"This is gonna sound weird, but did either of you just try to spook me by putting your hand on my shoulder?"

He was a paler shade of white.

"Of course not. We've been doing paper work right here on the kitchen table," I insisted.

"Don't bullshit me."

"Jerry, we swear. We didn't do it."

After a while he resumed work. Jerry slept in the living room that night over the area where the spots on the floor had formerly appeared. He slept with a Bible clutched in one hand and a doorknob Jesus tightly grasped in the other.

In the morning, he left. We never saw Jerry again.

The final straw occurred sometime later in the year. I worked at a Manhattan bank on weekends to earn a few extra dollars. Around noon on Saturday, I received a frantic call from Albert.

"Do you know where Phyllis's red rick rack ribbon is? I can't find it anywhere. I've torn apart the whole workroom!"

To help supplement our income, we also made custom items for our clients' interiors. Albert was working on a yellow shower curtain with red rick rack trim around the edges.

"Geez, I don't know. It was on the end of the bottom shelf behind the sewing machine."

I heard a loud noise in the background.

"What the hell was that?"

"Hold on. I'll be right back." He dropped he phone.

"What's wrong? Are you alright?" I said to no one.

I heard muffled cries of "fuck!" and "shit!" followed by mad stamping from and to the phone.

"There's fifty yards of red ribbon strewn all over the workroom. I'm outta here. We have to do something! I'll be at Dad's."

Albert left the flat immediately with yards and yards of red rick rack ribbon hanging from shelves, draped atop boxes, and caught in the window blinds. It was twisted around the chair in which he sat, wrapped around the sewing machine on which he worked. Turns out what really freaked him out was that twisted in the knots of ribbon around his chair were his large fabric shears.

It finally hit us that the atmosphere was twisting us into people fully aware and fully complicit in the story of this house. We were getting too used to this bit of continual theater, not unlike our landlord who became more and more evasive and distant.

We needed to solve this once and for all. Through an unfortunate marriage by his widowed father to a large-breasted manicurist affectionately known a "Big Tits," Albert had a step brother who, besides being a whiney opportunist, was a priest.

We decided to tolerate an evening with Father Henry, Albert's Dad, and Big Tits, and described the circumstances under which we were living. Over appetizers, we offered a condensed history of our experiences in the apartment.

"If what you're telling me is true," he said, "then your apartment will be classified by the church as a full blown possession."

"I see," Albert said.

"Don't worry," Father Henry said smugly, "I'd love to help you out with your little situation."

Even Father Henry, it seemed, had a high level of internal testosterone when it came to our apartment spirit. This surprised us because he never exhibited any strength about anything. We thought the doorknob Jesuses might have given him a combination of challenge and back up.

"I'd like to see the basement now," he said.

Albert led the way, followed by Father Henry and me. Albert's Dad and Big Tits remained upstairs with the dip and the crudité.

We no sooner reached the basement floor when Father Henry dropped like a stone, as if he'd suffered a massive attack. We all huddled around him and checked for his pulse. He woke within seconds, probably from the wailing of his mother.

We helped him upstairs, at which point he abruptly gathered up his belongings and made his way to the door. Big Tits and Albert's Dad had to run to catch up with him. He left for Rome shortly thereafter to the dismay of his Mother.

Our decision to move was more made *for* us than by us. Enough was enough. It didn't take us a long time to find a house that we loved in a neighborhood in which we felt comfortable. No renting, this time. We became home owners convinced that if we were going to struggle to pay for a place, then we might as well own it. Just prior to the closing, we brought in a medium to check out the karma of the house, not wanting to take any chances. If you can check the electrical and the plumbing, you can check the psychic atmosphere. It was all good.

Just prior to vacating the apartment, we remembered that we needed to return the scapulars to the nuns. We met the nun quintet for pizza, thanked each of them for the crosses, regaling in the stories of what went on. They nodded their heads in unison like Las Vegas back-up singers.

Upon returning home, we found that the urine stains in both areas on the floor had begun to grow again; gone were the doorknob Jesuses that had protected us. We moved within a week of rolling up the rug. The stains on the floor soon grew back to their original size, ready to engage the next unfortunate occupants.

EL DÍA DE LOS ANGELITOS INOCENTES

T.J. Lewes

MANY PEOPLE CELEBRATE THE DAY of the Dead, but in the town of Ocotepec, Mexico, the three days between October 31 and November 2 are the most important in the entire year. In that time, the veil to the spirit realm is lifted and deceased friends and relatives are invited home to visit. This past year, the ceremony was especially important to the Cruz family.

Señora Cruz was the first one up as always. She dressed in the dark before scurrying silently to the kitchen. Her mind raced with all the necessary preparations for the next three days, but her heart grieved that her home had given an Ofrenda Nueva that year.

Through the window, the first rays of dawn's glory caressed the wall over the side table, making the family photo hanging there glow vividly. In it, her twin sons sat front and center, while she and her husband stood proudly behind. Señora Cruz stopped and genuflected before turning away.

She began with the baking. El Pan de Muerto, bread of the dead, would take the entire day to prepare and decorate. She would make a whole skeleton this year in anticipation of hundreds of visitors. Once the dough was mixed, she covered it to let it rise, and set it in the corner. When she turned back around, she was overcome by the sight.

The end-of-October sun had risen completely over the Montezuma pines, and the morning light now baked the entire side table, making the objects on it shine. The candles seemed like they were lit, the marigolds looked like flames, the crepe paper decorations ap-

45

peared to be embers, and even the water was orange and glowing. The serapes danced in the rays as if alive, and the bowls of nuts and berries glistened. The effigy sitting below the picture was the only thing that didn't seem to be burning. The shadow it cast contrasted sharply with the blindingly bright light.

Once more Señora Cruz made the sign of the cross before returning to the cooking. By the time her husband and son wandered into the kitchen, the candied pumpkin was complete, the first dead bread was baking, tamales were wrapped to be cooked later, and breakfast was ready. The side-table looked resplendent, but no longer ethereal.

"Buenos días, Mamá. Diego's altar looks beautiful."

"Buenos días, Manuel. It'll look even better when we finish it tonight with the flowers you're going to collect today. Remember to gather lots of marigolds so we can make the petal path, and don't forget some carnations . . . they were Diego's favorite."

Manuel yawned widely, but nodded agreeably, as he sat down to eat his beans and rice. He would do anything to honor his brother. He had already picked three of his favorite things to add to the altar for the celebration that night.

Señor Cruz sat down too, but didn't touch his food. His sad eyes were glued to the family picture. Never before had he or his wife prepared to receive guests on November 1, El Día de Los Angelitos, although they had done so on November 2, El Día de Los Muertos, when their grandparents and parents had passed.

Señora Cruz didn't sit down. She pulled out the first loaves of long bone-shaped bread from the oven, and pushed a second tray of vertebrae into it. Then she set about shaping ribs from the dough. She didn't slow as she spoke.

"Hector, querido, I put a shopping list by the door. I still need to make the Atole and Sugar Skulls before tonight's service. I'll do the ponche tomorrow morning, but we need more incense please."

Without a word, Señor Cruz pushed aside his plate and rose to leave. His steps reverberated off the wooden floors and echoed down the adobe walls. Manuel jumped up to follow him, eager to get outside.

Enveloped in her silent kitchen, Señora Cruz began washing the dishes. Up until three months ago, Manuel and Diego always helped her. After Diego's sudden death, she didn't want to pressure Manuel with extra chores. Poor Manuel hadn't chuckled once since that fateful day; it was like his humor had died with Diego.

Images of Diego filled her mind; his explorative nature, his infectious laughter, his tousled hair . . . although her sons were identical twins, they had nearly opposite personalities. While Manuel was always cautious, polite, and obedient, Diego had been daring, impetuous, and mischievous, constantly pushing the hair out of his eyes to reveal the ragged scar on his temple from his first visit to the Church of El Divino Salvador de Ocotepec.

On that day at the Church, five years earlier when the boys were six, the difference in their personalities became crystal clear. During the Lord's Prayer, Manuel sat completely still with his eyes closed in perfect imitation of his mother's devotion, while Diego seized the opportunity to dash full speed down the central aisle. He tripped near the priest and fell headfirst into the stone baptismal font, which tumbled over, drenching him and gashing his forehead.

The congregation opened their eyes mid-Amen to a blood-covered, soaking wet, and screaming Diego. A few parishioners fainted, some made the sign of the cross, and others just glared. Father Navarro blessed the water and the child, over and over, as Señora Cruz ran to the altar, red-faced to retrieve her son. She rushed home cradling Diego as Manuel trudged dutifully behind.

The cut on Diego's temple was wide and the edges were abraded, but he did not suffer lasting impacts, other than the scar. Over the years, the wound had faded from dark red to nearly white. It was obvious against Diego's dark copper skin, so he always wore his long black bangs over that side.

Señora Cruz had prayed that he would learn temperance and self-control from his accident, but Diego considered himself invincible and became increasingly more reckless over the years. By age eleven, Diego thought he was already an adult and didn't need anyone's advice. He rarely did what he was told and even called his parents Mamí and Papí with the sarcastic inflection of a Latin Rapper.

Señor Cruz stomped in the front door. He was loaded with the ingredients on his wife's list, and he huffed into the kitchen visibly fatigued. Señora Cruz hurried to take the heavy bags from him. She brought him a glass of water and some fresh fruit cut on a plate. He gulped the water, but didn't eat.

"Isabel, I have decided to fast today in honor of our son. I will feast tonight with his spirit. Now I need to prepare the terrace. What I wouldn't give to have both my boys again."

With that, Señor Cruz went out the back door. His wife could hear him setting up the tables as she shaped the final mound of dough into a skull. She caressed the pliant mass, wishing instead she could stroke Diego's ebony locks.

"Vaya Diego, what I wouldn't give to hold you again."

Her eyes rested on the effigy. It was made of gourds, grasses, sticks, plantains, and corn, but dressed in a brand-new suit and tie, with shiny black shoes. It seemed more like a person masquerading as food than food dressed as a person. Señora Cruz shuddered and genuflected once more before beginning the Sugar Skulls.

While Hector and Isabel Cruz readied the house, Manuel wandered through the hills and meadows surrounding the village in search of flowers. He had already picked over one-hundred marigolds, but he hadn't found any carnations yet. He decided to climb down into the valley, where a small stream meandered through the dense and rocky underbrush.

After nearly an hour of scrambling along the bank, Manuel stumbled across a field of vibrant red carnations, not far from the old stone bridge. He picked dozens before approaching the stream to grab some of the lilies nestled there. He noticed his reflection out of the corner of his eyes. A rock under the surface left a jagged edge along his temple, transforming his likeness. For a moment, Manuel saw his brother vividly in the murky water, lunging toward him. He leapt back away from the edge, the lilies still clasped in his shaking hands.

On his long walk home, Manuel thought of his brother and the events that led to his demise. In July, the twins had gone out to explore the hills surrounding Ocotepec. Mother had warned them many times about the bridge leading to the foothills along the west.

"Remember mis amores, always be careful on the old stone bridge. The rocks are slippery and sometimes fall loose. Stay off the side barrier rails and walk only in the middle."

Manuel had taken her advice seriously, but Diego considered it a challenge. When the boys arrived at the bridge, Diego jumped up onto the side wall, which was also made of slick, crumbling rocks. Manuel walked straight down the middle, with his eyes focused directly in front of him, trying to ignore Diego's taunts.

"You're such a wimp! I'm gonna call you Manuela from now on, for being such a girl. Look at Manuela, the proper princess prancing ov—"

Manuel did not see his brother slip, but he heard the groan Diego made as he hit the railing. Manuel turned his head to see Diego clinging to the side, his feet dangling precariously over the ravine. Feeling vindicated, Manuel laughed before reaching out his hand. It was too late. The stone Diego was clinging to dislodged, plummeting him down into rocky chasm.

On one hand, Manuel recognized that it was Diego's stubborn bravado that caused his death, but on the other, Manuel felt responsible and guilty. If he had just moved faster, perhaps Diego would be with them right now. If he hadn't laughed at his brother before trying to help, maybe he could have saved him.

"Oh Diego, I'm so sorry. What I wouldn't give to have you here again."

When Manuel arrived home, it was late afternoon. Señor Cruz was busy sweeping the front walkway and Señora Cruz was putting the final touches on her bread skeleton. She stopped as soon as Manuel came through the door.

"Gracias a Dios, Manuel. I was worried something had happened to you! Are you ok? Did you get all the flowers?"

Manuel smiled politely and opened his sack. "Está bien Mamá. The carnations were farther away than I expected, but now we have some lilies too."

"Oh Manuel, you are such a good boy. Here, let me feed you. You must be famished."

Manuel sank gratefully into the chair as his mom bustled around the kitchen preparing a quick meal of tortilla, salad, fresh fruit, and the left-over beans and rice. As Manuel ate, she unpacked the flowers, placing the carnations and lilies in water on the altar before settling onto a chair to de-petal the marigolds. Shortly later, Manuel and his father joined her to help.

When all the flowers had been plucked bare, Manuel retreated to his room to prepare for the evening's service. Like every year, he and his parents had gone to Church daily since October 18, the day of Ocotepec's Patron Saint Luke. Although Manuel had never minded the nearly constant novena in honor of the deceased, this year he suffered.

Manuel dressed extra-carefully for the evening's activities. October 31 was the night to welcome the spirits of deceased children: Los Angelitos Inocentes, the Innocent Little Angels. As an Ofrenda Nueva, new offering from the previous year, Diego's spirit would surely come. Everything had to be perfect.

Señor and Señora Cruz also prepared themselves carefully. Before leaving, Señora Cruz packed a large basket of food, drinks, blankets, and candles while Manuel placed three very special items on his brother's altar: his soccer ball, his favorite race car, and the beautiful piece of quartz that Diego always coveted.

Señora Cruz and Manuel walked out the front door, down the garden path, and to the sidewalk. Señor Cruz followed, spreading marigold petals carefully behind him. The path of petals extended from the altar in the kitchen all the way to the sidewalk. He left the front door open.

A large group was forming on the street outside. Neighbors, all carrying satchels or baskets, swept down the street, pulling the Cruz family in their tide. The procession ended at the cemetery, each family settling in around the ornate miniature churches that covered the graves of their deceased relatives.

Señora Cruz spread a large blanket over Diego's gravesite as Señor Cruz lit candles at the four corners of Diego's brightly tiled structure. In the candlelight, the mosaic seemed to dance and sway. Although many families laughed and talked, the Cruz family ate in silence until Señor Perez arrived, his booming voice breaking the somber vigil.

"Buenas noches, Hector and Isabel. What a big night for your family. Manuel, how are you my dear god-son?"

Señor Perez settled onto the blanket next to Manuel, his hand briskly patting the boy's back. Manuel nodded, and smiled slightly in greeting, but didn't speak. Soon Señora Perez joined them, a wrapped package in her hands.

"Hola Isabel. ¿Qué anda Hector? I have some things for Diego's altar. Javier and I will bring it over tonight before the midnight bells."

"Gracias Luisa, you are an angel", Señora Cruz said as she prepared extra plates of food for Señor and Señora Perez.

Soon the four adults were engrossed in conversation about

preparations for the following day. By custom, the entire town would congregate in the cemetery in the morning to honor the deceased children. Throughout the day, everyone in town would be coming to the Cruz household to pay their respects and to celebrate Diego. Manuel sat silently watching the candlelight dance on his brother's monument. The flickering light was hypnotic and seemed to waver in rhythm to Manuel's thoughts.

"It's my fault that Diego died. I should have paid attention. I knew the danger even if he didn't. I'm responsible. I'm guilty. I'm the one who should be dead."

Father Navarro's voice pulled Manuel out of his trance. His tall, robed figure stood in the center of the cemetery, an incense burner in one hand and a candle in the other. The time had come to open the gate for the spirits.

"We are gathered here this evening to welcome home the spirits of our dear children who have passed beyond. May their journey home be sacred and may their families be blessed. En el nombre del Padre, del Hijo, y del Espíritu Santo. Let us pray. Our Father who art in Heaven, hallowed be Thy name, Thy kingdom come, Thy will be done, on Earth as it is in Heaven, give us today our daily bread, and forgive us our trespasses . . ."

Goosebumps broke out on Manuel's arms. Would Diego forgive him?

". . . as we forgive those that trespass against us, and lead us not into temptation, but deliver us from evil."

Manuel felt a hand upon his shoulder. He reached up, eyes still closed, to grasp the hand, but nothing was there. He trembled and held his breath.

"For Thine is the kingdom, the power, and the glory. Am–"

"Fuego!"

Manuel didn't know who screamed, but he opened his eyes to see the edge of their blanket on fire. The flames were running quickly toward him. He jumped up, grabbed the canteen, and doused the blanket as his parents and god-parents tried to salvage the offerings and food. Then Manuel stomped the smoking fabric until he was sure the fire was out completely.

Manuel assumed that one of the candles must have fallen over, but when the thick smoke cleared, all four candles at the corners of the mini-chapel were still lit. At the end of the service, the

Cruz family packed up quietly and said nothing on the walk home. Señor and Señora Perez joined them in their silent march.

The moon had risen over the hilltops when they arrived at the Cruz household. The light it cast made everything look two-dimensional, except for the path of marigold petals, which seemed to float above the ground. Hector and Isabel Cruz walked down the path first, followed by Luisa and Javier Perez. Manuel followed behind, the hair on the back of his neck bristling.

Señores Cruz and Perez retired to the back terrace while their wives remained with Manuel in the kitchen. Señora Cruz readied the final pieces of the altar. She added Diego's favorite foods, rice pudding, and a large avocado, as well as several trinkets and his baptism certificate. Señora Perez opened the carefully wrapped package she had brought.

First, she pulled out a new Bible. In the candlelight, its leather cover gleamed and its gilded pages glowed. She laid it next to the effigy. The second item was a wooden rosary, which she placed on top of the Bible. Finally, she pulled out a small stone statue that had been shaped into a likeness of Diego. The similarity was incredible, down to the scar on his right temple. Señora Cruz stared at the statuette for several moments before speaking.

"Mil gracias, Luisa. Where did you get such a beautiful statue?"

"From Señor Alvarez. His stonework is legendary, but this piece is his finest work."

Señora Perez caressed the statue. It had cost nearly a month's income, but her god-son deserved the best. Manuel looked at the altar with a heavy heart. He began to think that everyone loved Diego more than him.

The church bells started ringing, their metallic chimes echoing off the surrounding hills and barreling back through the quiet streets and houses, until all of Ocotepec vibrated with the sound. Señores Cruz and Perez joined their wives in the kitchen before the last notes faded from the night. Together, they all bowed their heads in prayer. Señor Cruz had spent the day planning his speech.

"Bien venido, Diego. We have opened our hearts and home to your spirit. We have created an altar for your soul, with candles for fire, bread for earth, crepe paper for air, and our finest bowl filled with water. We have laid the marigold path for your arrival. Please honor us with your presence, please accept our offerings, and please know our undying love. We miss you, my son."

Manuel shifted uncomfortably. Long after Señor and Señora Perez had gone, and his parents had retired to bed, Manuel's mind repeated one question over and over: Would they miss me as much? He tossed and turned in bed for hours, until finally drifting to sleep after 3:00 AM. He awoke to his mother's calls.

"Manuel, levántate . . . Manuel, we need to leave soon for the cemetery . . . Manuel!"

"Coming Mamá."

The exhausted boy rolled out of bed and dressed quickly. By the time he had used the bathroom and brushed his teeth and hair, his father was yelling from sidewalk.

"Manuel, apúrate. We must leave now!"

Manuel rushed outside, careful not to disturb the petals, and joined the morning procession to the graveyard. Neither of his parents wished him a good morning. In fact, they seemed annoyed at his tardiness.

The Cruz family was one of the last to enter the cemetery. Aunts, uncles, cousins, and his god-parents were all huddled around Diego's site. Like the previous evening, Señora Cruz laid out their blanket while Señor Cruz lit the candles in each corner of the memorial chapel. Manuel took a seat as far away from the monument as he could.

A full Catholic Mass was said that morning by Father Navarro, but Manuel heard little of it. He was too focused on his internal dialogue to hear God's word. Guilt fed on his soul, responsibility laid on his shoulders, and feelings of worthlessness tormented his spirit. If he wasn't sitting, his legs would have given out from the weight.

After Mass, the Cruz family returned home quickly to prepare for visitors. Señora Cruz made a hot fruit punch called ponche, brewed coffee, set out her elaborate dead bread skeleton, and began cooking the tamales she had prepared the day before. Manuel helped his father perfect the arrangement of tables and chairs on the back terrace and then reported to the kitchen to help his mother with guests. Before long, the first of many visitors arrived.

Father Navarro was still dressed in his ceremonial robes. At nearly seventy years old, his silver hair glistened in the morning light as he strode down the marigold path to the altar. Without so much as a glance at Manuel, Father Navarro began a prayer for Diego's spirit. When he finished, he lit a candle and placed it on the altar with his blessings.

Father Navarro accepted a cup of ponche and a piece of foot, before retiring outside to chat with Señor Cruz. Manuel sat silently inside at the kitchen table, staring at the candle on the altar. Would Father Navarro be the first to light a memorial candle for him?

The Gonzalez family from next door appeared before Manuel could think farther. All nine of them lit candles and laid flowers on the altar. Each person shared a fond memory before taking their refreshments outside to the terrace. Their kind words assaulted Manuel.

"Diego was so funny, he could always make me laugh."

"Remember when Diego was four and he left our fence gate open and all of our chickens ran down the road? What a time to get them back. I will never forget that dear boy!"

"Remember when he tried to give flowers to Tía Rosa, but a huge spider was inside the bouquet? I never saw Rosa move so fast in my life! What a golden memory Diego gave us."

"Remember the time he went to get the water, but forgot to take a pitcher with him so he borrowed the one Señora Ramirez had in her front yard? She called the police so many times that they threatened her with charges of harassment and dropped their investigation. I don't think she ever got her pitcher back!"

Every comment was said with laughter. Just thinking about Diego brought happiness to those he touched. Manuel wondered what stories people would tell of him? His hair was always combed neatly? He got good grades at school? He picked nice flowers?

Manuel hung his head and sat without word the entire day, listening as visitors shared their fond recollections. Each story that lifted Diego up pushed Manuel farther down into the depths of his depression. He did not eat, drink, or speak.

As the sun set on the last of the over three-hundred visitors that day, Señora Cruz prepared the basket for that evening's feast at the cemetery. Only a clavicle and the skull remained from her dead bread. She placed them on the altar before rushing to get ready for the evening's procession.

Manuel sat alone in the kitchen with his brother's altar. Nearly sixty candles were still burning. Half of the kitchen glowed brightly while the other half was drenched in flickering darkness. A few candles behind the statue burned strong, sending a dark likeness of Diego onto the side wall. The wavering candles made the shadow appear to be moving.

A crash from next to the altar pulled Manuel's attention away from the shadow. He stood and approached the altar carefully. On the floor, he found the fragments of his piece of quartz. Nervously, he swept up the shards with his hands, wondering how the rock he placed at the back of the altar could have shattered in front of it.

Manuel shivered as a cold draft rippled over his skin and left the kitchen quickly to get ready for Church. He didn't want to be late again. Soon the entire Cruz family was assembled in the kitchen, washed, dressed, and packed.

Many of the candles had gone out, but the ones behind the statue still burned brightly. Diego's shadow was even more distinct, large and looming by the hallway. Señora Cruz crossed herself, Señor Cruz bowed his head and said a quick prayer, and Manuel held his breath. They all hurried outside.

They arrived at the cemetery early to set up their final offering to Diego. Señora Cruz readied the blanket, food, and gifts, while Señor Cruz attended to the candles. In addition to the ones at each corner, he made an extra cross of candles pointing the spirit back home. He loved Diego very much, but knew that his spirit should not stay. El Día de Los Angelitos Inocentes was coming to an end.

Soon the relatives joined the Cruz family at the cemetery. Together they all feasted, again sharing pleasant recollections and statements of honor for Diego. Manuel did not join in the conversation or the feast, but he did pray to his brother the entire time.

"Diego, dear brother, you are loved by all who knew you. You are cherished by all you touched. I am nothing compared to you. Please forgive me and help me make this right."

By the time the Cruz family returned home, Manuel had sunk to the bottom of his personal torment. He sat on a chair in the kitchen facing the altar while his parents prepared for the activities of the following day. Since no adult had passed from their home in the previous year, no visitors would be coming, but the Cruz family would be paying respects at the homes of others in town. They packed bags of candles, tequila, and flowers as offerings to take along.

When the midnight bells chimed the end of El Día de Angelitos Inocentes and the beginning of El Día de Muertos, the Cruz family held hands around the table. Señor Cruz cleared his throat. When he spoke, his voice was thick with emotion.

"Te queremos, Diego. From the bottom of our hearts, we all love and miss you. We adore you and the joy you brought us. We wish you a safe journey home, my son, and look forward to celebrating with you again next year. We hope our offerings have been enough, and pray your spirit is at peace. Adiós, Mijo."

Señor and Señora Cruz wished Manuel a good night before retiring to bed, leaving the boy sitting alone in the kitchen. The last candles burning were the ones behind the statue and the shadow cast was an inky black on the adobe wall. Manuel thought it seemed like the shadow was moving toward him, but figured it must be a trick of the light. He laid his weary head on the table and fell asleep within moments. He was still there sleeping when Señora Cruz bustled into the kitchen the following morning.

"Goodness my son, someone is up before me? That's a miracle. Have you been there all night?"

The boy raised his head slowly and laughed, his messy hair hanging into his eyes. When he brushed the hair back off his forehead, Señora Cruz glimpsed a white scar on his temple.

"Sí, Mamí. I've been here all night."

Señora Cruz fainted, rousing Señor Cruz with the crash she made on the floor. He rushed down the hall, into the kitchen, to find his son kneeling next to her as she began to regain consciousness. Señor Cruz hurried to her side, his voice loud with fear as he questioned his son.

"Qué pasó hijo?"

"I don't know. She came into the kitchen, asked me a question, then collapsed. I think she passed out."

Señora Cruz opened her eyes and stared around the room confused, until focusing on the concerned face of her husband. He held her hand and helped her sit up on the floor. His voice shook.

"Isabel, ¿Está bien? What happened?"

Before answering her husband, Señora Cruz looked at her son carefully. His brow was etched with concern, but seemed scar free. She decided that it must have been a trick of the morning light and shadow.

"I'm sorry I scared you my loves. I think I need some water and a hearty breakfast to get my strength back. The last couple days have been challenging for all of us."

Señor Cruz helped his wife to a chair, then brought her a glass of water as Manuel offered to help make breakfast. Señora Cruz waved her husband and son away to get dressed for the morning's Mass at the cemetery so she could cook and pack the basket. They had another full day of honoring the dead ahead of them.

Before cooking, Señora Cruz sat at the table, her mind reeling. She was sure Manuel had called her Mamí, just like Diego. The boy had laughed, just like Diego. And by God, she was certain she had seen the scar!

She shook her head to clear it, then lumbered to the counter to prepare the morning meal. Soon the town would file into the cemetery one last time for Mass. She finished making breakfast just as her husband joined her in the kitchen.

"Are you sure you're okay, Isabel?"

"Yes, yes, of course. Ummm . . . where is Manuel?"

"Still in his room. I'll go get him."

Señor Cruz wandered down the hall to the bedroom the twins shared. Manuel's belongings were on the left, Diego's were still on the right. Señor Cruz was surprised to see his son standing in front of Diego's dresser.

"Manuel, it's time to eat."

"Ay, Papí."

The boy, dressed in Diego's clothes, smirked as he turned. He pushed past his father and flew down the hall. He was already eating when Señor Cruz sat down. The man's eyes were wide and a slight sweat sheened his forehead. He seemed pale. Señora Cruz looked at her husband oddly.

"Hector, is everything okay?"

"All is well dear. Let's eat and go to Mass."

The Cruz family ate quickly and joined the processional to the cemetery. The morning had dawned gray and overcast. A sinewy fog enveloped the town and the congregants. When they entered the graveyard, instead of heading to Diego's plot, they went to the graves of the Cruz and Suarez families' ancestors, in the far back corner. Señora Cruz laid flowers and food offerings at the site of each relative, while Señor Cruz lit a single candle in front of each small, tile chapel.

Soon aunts, uncles, and cousins joined them in remembrance of their loved ones, each bringing offerings. Nearly fifty relatives congregated together; only Manuel was missing. He, alone, stood in the children's section of the graveyard, head downturned, staring at Diego's monument, his uncombed hair falling into his eyes.

Señor and Señora Cruz noticed Manuel's odd behavior. The extended family commented on it several times. Even Father Navarro made note of the strange occurrence. Something wasn't right.

The Mass for El Día de Muertos that morning consecrated the spirits of deceased adults. It honored their lives, and sanctified their deaths. The Lord's Prayer was spoken in unison by the hundreds of people packed into the cemetery. Their words carried on the wisps of gray clouds that cloaked them. Manuel remained alone at Diego's site the entire time. With the thick, undulating fog, Manuel's body seemed to disappear and reappear.

At the end of the service, after most of the parishioners were gone, Señor and Señora Cruz joined Manuel at Diego's grave. He stood motionless as they approached him from behind. Señora Cruz called out to him quietly.

"Manuel, mi amor."

The boy didn't move. It was as if he didn't hear her speaking. Señor Cruz tried next, his voice loud and strong.

"Manuel, it's time to go."

Again, the boy was oblivious. He remained statue still. Father Navarro joined the Cruz family, his hand up signaling silence to the parents as he approached. After making the sign of the cross and clutching his rosary tightly, the priest walked up to the boy and whispered into his ear.

"Diego."

The boy whipped around. He laughed loudly, then sprinted down the path, out of the graveyard, and toward the western hills. Señor and Señora Cruz clasped hands and watched him run through the mist, remaining in the cemetery in discussion with Father Navarro for several minutes.

When they finally left the graveyard, it was nearly midday. Father Navarro and the Cruzes all knew how much needed to be done in the next twelve hours. The gate to the spirit realm would close at midnight.

As soon as they arrived home, Señor Cruz set about dismantling Diego's altar. The only things he didn't touch were Manuel's soccer ball and race car, and the marigold pathway. He put the candles on the counter for later use, emptied the water, cleaned the bowl, threw away the bread and food offerings, and burned the crepe paper decorations, Bible, rosary, and flowers in the fire pit.

Señora Cruz joined him on the back terrace, her arms full of Diego's old clothes from the bedroom. Señor Cruz sighed deeply, but added them to the flames. Little by little, the grieving parents burned all of Diego's possessions, until only Manuel's items, and the furniture, remained in the bedroom.

Together they wrestled Diego's bed outside and burned that, too. The flames were higher than their rooftop. When they added Diego's dresser, Señora Cruz was certain that the fires of Hell could not be more intense. They held hands and bowed their heads in prayer, Señor Cruz intoning the oration.

"Dear Father, we have freed Diego from the bonds to our world. Please guide his spirit back to you where it belongs. We release him into your heavenly arms. In your name, we pray. Amen."

Together, Señor and Señora Cruz threw the effigy into the middle of the inferno. They held each other, crying openly, until the last charred remains had disappeared in the blaze. Together, they returned to the kitchen to gather their offerings. Time for visiting.

The Cruzes first paid their respects at the Sanchez household. Señor Sanchez had been a good friend. When he passed in the spring, many grieved him, and nearly forty friends and relatives were relaxing at his house. After lighting candles, offering tequila, and laying flowers on the altar, both Señor and Señora Cruz took a moment to talk quietly with the other visitors. Their message was simple.

"Please come to the cemetery tonight at ten. Manuel needs you."

They repeated their activities at the homes of the other three new offerings. By the time they finished visiting, it was late afternoon, and they had spoken to at least half of the town's residents. They rushed to the market to purchase new items for an effigy—premade crepe paper decorations, a large golden candle, and bread. On the way home, they purchased several bouquets of flowers.

Together, the exhausted parents built a new altar and effigy for Manuel. Instead of wrapping the effigy in the traditional suit and tie, they dressed it a comfortable jogging suit and sneakers; clothes they prayed Manuel would wear the following day. They added the paper, a bowl of fresh water, and the bread. Father Navarro arrived to light the large, golden candle, first to say a prayer for the kind-hearted boy.

"Manuel, you are a special son of God and an honor to man. In Jesus's name, we pray for your safety and offer our love. By the power invested in me, I bless this altar as a doorway for your return. Come to us. Amen."

Señor and Señora Cruz each lit a candle and placed it on the altar. They leaned into each other for support. Although their voices shook, they spoke loudly to assure that they would be heard in the spirit realm.

"Manuel, you have always been such a blessing. You have made me a very proud father. Every day I find something new to admire in you. Please come back Manuel. I want to know the man you become."

"Mijo, no mother could ask for more than a son like you. I love you with all my heart and pray that you will return home to me. We beg you to hear us and come back!"

The sky glowed red as Señor and Señora Cruz followed Father Navarro to the old stone bridge. They carried Diego's stone statue with them, wrapped tightly in the serape from his altar. The serape was the only piece of Diego's clothing they hadn't burned, other than the outfit Manuel was wearing.

Father Navarro strode down the path invigorated, like a man forty years younger. Although his face was drawn with concern, his eyes shone with passion. He carried a large satchel with him, its contents rattling dissonantly as he stepped. Señor and Señora Cruz struggled to keep up with him, and soon fell behind. Señora Cruz held her husband's arm tightly.

"Hector, I'm scared. I don't want to do this. I don't want to go to the bridge where Diego died!"

"Isabel, either we face Diego's death, or we are responsible for Manuel's. We must do this."

"But Hector, we already burned everything, why must we destroy the beautiful statue too?"

"Because Father Navarro said so. We must trust him, Isabel."

Father Navarro realized that the Cruzes had fallen far behind, but he did not stop until he reached the foot of the bridge. When Señor and Señora Cruz finally arrived, he had already laid out the contents of his bag and was praying over the items. There were candles, a container of ashes, a flask of holy water, a Bible, and a knife. He held the ornately carved copper incense burner in his right hand, swinging it back and forth on its long chain. After his throaty Amen, Father Navarro placed the burner on the ground and turned to the parents.

"Let me have Diego's statue now. We must bless it and preserve his spirit, before you throw it over the bridge."

Señora Cruz cradled the bundle in her arms, before reluctantly handing it to Father Navarro. He unwrapped the statue from the serape, handling it carefully, like a newborn. He spread the serape on the ground, placed the statue in the center, then lit a candle in each direction; north, south, east, then finally west. The flame on the western candle blended seamlessly into the setting sun behind it.

Father Navarro kneeled in front of the statue, motioning the parents to join him, one on each side. He used the holy water to bless Diego's spirit, anointing the statue with it. Together they recited the Lord's Prayer, before Father Navarro drew an ash cross on each of their foreheads to protect them. He placed the holy water in his pocket, and lifted the knife.

"It is time to add our blood to Diego's statue, to help free his spirit from our world."

Señor Cruz held out his hand to Father Navarro. The priest nicked Hector's thumb with the gilded knife. A single, large drop of blood formed on the man's upturned pad. Father Navarro pulled Hector's hand over the statue, tilting it so that the blood dropped onto Diego's stone head.

Father Navarro repeated the ritual on a very nervous Señora Cruz, before cutting himself. Using his bleeding thumb, he made a blood cross on the statue's forehead, careful to obscure the carved scar completely. Then he turned to face the bridge.

The setting sun had nearly disappeared behind the hill. The ravine below the bridge was already enveloped in darkness, and the bridge itself glowed slightly in the remaining, ambient light. Father Navarro genuflected before striding to the center of the bridge. He beckoned the Cruzes to join him.

Slowly, Señor Cruz shuffled onto the stones, his trembling wife pressed up to his back. Neither of them had been to the bridge since Diego's fall. Señor Cruz felt like he could hardly breathe, but his feet took him to Father Navarro's side.

"Hector, you and Isabel must be the ones to throw Diego's statue over the side. I can only serve as Guardian . . . you must free the spirit."

Father Navarro handed the statue to Señor Cruz. He held it gingerly and looked at his wife, her tear-stained cheeks glistening in the final rays. Holding hands, they approached the side rail, careful of their footing. Señor Cruz whispered a final goodbye to their son.

"Diego, we love you and miss you, but the time has come for you to go to your spiritual home. Our world is no longer open to you. Take your rightful place in the spirit world now. Adiós Hijo, go to God."

Señor Cruz held the head of the statue, while Señora Cruz took the feet. It lay between them, like a sleeping child reposed upon the air. They swung it back and forth three times before hurtling it into space off the side of the bridge.

"NO!"

A dark figure ran onto the opposite side of the bridge, screaming loudly. His arm was outstretched and his face was contorted in fury and anguish. A white scar glinted on his temple.

Señor and Señora Cruz huddled together, petrified. As they inched their way backwards, Father Navarro stepped forward to face the enraged boy. The priest held the Bible in front of him like a shield, and began an oration for protection.

"Bendito Salvador, protégenos contra las fuerzas de . . . "

The boy approached them in the middle of the bridge, laughing. His cackle was loud and harsh, more like a growl than a snicker. It drowned out the old priest's prayer. When the boy spoke, his words dripped with contempt.

"You think a prayer and some ash can protect you? You think you can get rid of me just by burning some stuff and throwing away a statue? I plan to stay with my dear Mamí and Papí forever. If they don't want me to remain here, I'll just take them back with me."

Diego turned to face his shaking parents. His dark eyes seemed to glow. He reached his hands out toward them as he stepped forward, a predatory smile on his face.

Thump.

Diego's limp body fell to the ground. Father Navarro stood behind him, the heavy metal butt of the knife sticking out of his wrapped fist. The priest dropped the blade and sank to the ground, as shocked as the Cruzes. Señora Cruz was the first to regain her senses.

She ran to her son first to verify that he was still alive, then attended to Father Navarro. The priest had never struck another human being in his entire life, and remained sitting on the bridge in a state of stupefaction. After several failed attempts to get the priest to focus, Señora Cruz smacked him squarely on the cheek.

It worked. Father Navarro leapt to his feet, retrieved his knife, and strode over to the boy's unconscious body. His voice was firm as he gave directions.

"We must tie your son and carry him to the cemetery. We cannot let him escape. There is not much time left. Hurry!"

Father Navarro retrieved several lengths of rope from his satchel. Together, the priest and the parents bound the lad's wrists and ankles. Señor Cruz insisted on carrying the boy himself, hoisting him across his shoulders. He walked slowly, but made it all the way to the cemetery.

Señora Cruz walked with her husband, while Father Navarro rushed ahead to make final arrangements for the impromptu exorcism. The priest prayed enough people would come–Manuel would need the support of the entire village to beat Diego's spirit. He patted his pocket to assure the holy water was with him.

By the time the Cruz family arrived shortly after ten, the whole graveyard glowed with candles, each held by a loving relative, friend, and neighbor. Word had spread throughout the village about Manuel's need for help, and everyone had come to assist the dear boy. The congregation had circled around Diego's tomb-site, leaving space for the Cruz family in the middle.

Father Navarro helped Señor Cruz lower the unconscious boy, who stirred when he hit the ground, but did not awaken. The crowd murmured its surprise at the bonds and pressed closer together, beginning to understand the gravity of the situation. The morning's fog had returned that evening. It was dense and dark, pushing down on the inhabitants. Looking around the circle, Señora Cruz could barely make out the faces surrounding her. Each candle looked like a glowing orb suspended in air. She shuddered.

Father Navarro stood between the boy and Diego's monument. He first blessed the site with his incense, then arranged a candle cross beside him. When he was sure the site had been prepared, he began that evening's ceremony.

"Ladies and gentlemen, we are gathered here this evening to retrieve the soul of our lost lamb Manuel. His spirit has been displaced by that of his brother. We must send Diego to the Holy Father, and bring Manuel back to us. We have already broken all of Diego's ties to our world, but now we must invite Manuel back. I need each of you to share your fondest recollection of Manuel, so that he can know his value here among us."

Señora Gonzalez was the first to speak out. "We all remember when Diego let all our chickens escape, but what I remember is that it was Manuel who helped me gather them back. Manuel is a treasure."

Señora Ramirez stepped forward next. "If it wasn't for dear Manuel, I would never have gotten my grandmother's pitcher back. I nearly died of heart break when it went missing. After the police refused to help, I gave up hope of ever seeing it again. Manuel alone got it back for me. He will never know how much that meant to me!"

One by one, the parishioners shared their tales of Manuel's kindness and generosity. They praised his beautiful spirit and his willingness to help. Señor Perez was the last to speak.

"I love Manuel. He is so much more to me than just my godson. Every visit I knew he would teach me something. He found the world amazing, and through his eyes I did, too."

The boy on the ground growled. Although he was still bound, he lumbered onto his feet. Then he turned his head to stare at Señor Perez, before hissing a reply.

"The only thing Manuel knew about was plants and rocks. He was weak. He was nothing compared to me, and he knew it!"

Señor Perez shrunk back into the mist, visibly shaken. The congregation huddled tighter together. Father Navarro spoke next.

"Diego, you are not welcome here. Leave this body and this world. Return to the spirit realm. The ancestors are calling you back to them now!"

Father Navarro doused Diego with the holy water. The boy fell back onto ground, writhing and yelling, as the water burned his skin. Father Navarro raised his voice over the wails.

"Manuel, our lost Angel, you are the kindest among us. Always the first to help, always the last to give up, always the one to follow the path of righteousness. We love you! We need you! Come back to us now!"

The entire congregation spoke the Lord's Prayer as the midnight bells tolled the end of el Día de Muertos. Over three-hundred people yelled Amen, the echo riding on the last bell toll. Silence.

Señora Cruz rushed to the boy's side. He was curled in a fetal position, completely still. She hesitantly touched his shoulder and whispered.

"Manuel, mi amor, are you ok?"

The boy raised his head slowly, revealing his smooth forehead and tearful eyes. His voice was weak.

"Sí Mamá. I think I am."

As the town of Ocotepec cheered, Señor Cruz and Father Navarro helped Manuel to his feet, releasing his bonds. The boy was unsteady, but stood proudly as several friends and relatives wished him well on their way out. Father Navarro accompanied the Cruz family home.

When Manuel entered the kitchen, he was overwhelmed by the altar there. The large gold candle still flickered in the middle, flanked by the smaller ones his parents had dedicated. The effigy, wearing Manuel's new track suit, was surrounded by several bouquets of flowers. It looked like the entire stock of the local florist was on the side table.

"Mamá, can we keep the flowers? It smells wonderful in here."

"Of course, my dear. The track suit is for you as well. Here, let me help you get it off the effigy."

"Gracias Mamá. Gracias Papá. Buenas Noches, Father Navarro."

Manuel cradled the new jogging suit tight to his chest as he wandered down the hall to bed, his father following. He could barely recognize his bedroom. With only his furniture, the room seemed huge.

"Manuel, please change into your pajamas and give me the clothes you are wearing."

Manuel looked down at himself, surprised. He hadn't realized he was wearing Diego's clothes. He rushed to get into his pajamas, then offered the clothes to his father, before crawling wearily into bed. He fell asleep almost immediately.

Señor Cruz joined his wife and Father Navarro in the kitchen, carrying the bundle of clothing. Together the three adults retired to the back terrace, lighting one more Día de Muertos fire in the pit. They watched the last of Diego's possessions burn in silence. When the final threads had burned to ash, Father Navarro sprinkled the remaining drops of holy water onto the smoking mass before taking his leave. The priest had never been more exhausted in his life.

After locking up for the night, Señor and Señora Cruz crept down the hall to Manuel's doorway. The boy was sleeping soundly, bathed in the moonlight. His soft snores made Señor Cruz smile broadly, but they made his wife cry.

"What's wrong Isabel? It is done. Manuel is safe now!"

"Now, yes. But tell me Hector, what about next year?"

The poor man had no answer.

THE TIBETAN ADDRESS BOOK OF THE DEAD

Judith Speizer Crandell

Prologue: Epilogue

A NEW ONE HAS DIED. Cross him off. Cross him off. They can bury him, including the following items: an entire 89-year-old male skeletal system; desiccated pale flesh; an unlit fat cigar; red hair gone gray, gone entirely; the right fender of a hot red 1965 Cadillac Coupe De Ville; a broken axle of a 1968 Chevy Impala death-trap bluebird-blue convertible; two round-trip tickets to Miami Beach; a moth-eaten faded green sweater; two dried roses; three sheets of address labels from Livingston, New Jersey.

Living-stone. Address of the House of Horrors he erected along with his bride of Frankenstein. But he is dead. No longer alive. No longer able to scream bloody murder. No longer able to piss or eat ham steaks and baby lamb chops while the rest of the family ate hamburgers and hotdogs because it was *his* money, you'd better know it was *his* goddamned money, after all, that paid for everything that went into your goddamned mouth, everything that clothed your goddamned naked body. Rachel's naked body. The one he secretly and not-so secretly wanted to possess.

His money, his house, his show, his children. He sucked the life out of the stepchildren, the ones he made his. They weren't his. Even though the lawyers listed them with his birth children and surviving wife. He used a plastic flexi-straw to do the sucking. Remember those? What would it take to award him post-death an Academy

Award for Best Actor in the Category of Vampires?

He is inscribed in Rachel's book of the dead, along with the others. He is a real stand-out because of the bad-ass-karma-will-likely-return-to-earth life he had lived this time around. But, dear Rachel, like so many others in this decrepit address book you use to call home, he is dead. Isn't it time to execute spring cleaning?

# # #

Rachel knows you can tell if someone is dead, really dead: They don't call you back in a reasonable amount of time; don't show up at work, but haven't quit; never answer a letter or an email for a long, long time; have no earthly address anymore; don't talk to people they love; don't scream at people they hate; and, the one sign she learned by watching *Hill Street Blues*, they don't leave a filmy mist on a mirror held up to their mouths—now that's a "dead" giveaway.

While Rachel has a less-than-minor understanding of the ancient *Tibetan Book of the Dead*, she thinks the stages are helpful markers, like a stop sign or a detour sign or a bump sign or better yet, a yield sign. Rachel once stole a pedestrian crossing sign with the long-haired guy who was her college boyfriend and, unfortunately, went on to become her husband for seven years. She liked the double entendre of "pedestrian." Being rather literal and mostly into race cars and sex with produce, he just liked stealing the sign.

Rachel can be funny, really funny, even when she tries to be serious, as she has tried to be with this dead book, this book of the dead. She took notes, printing neatly so she could read her own writing. She put down in block letters the important "R" words she found because there were so many of them like "REBIRTH," "REVEAL," "RESUSSITATE," "REVEAL," "RESURRECT," "REMEMBER," "REVEAL," and "REGURGITATE." She failed to notice that "REVEAL" was listed three times.

Then she inscribed into her half-writing, half-sketching journal for the Brooklyn Art Project, her *Book of Life*, the following words:

I don't want to be blasphemous, to insult the true believers, the true gurus. But at this point in my existence, I find their systematic way of framing the passage from one incarnation to the next very helpful. I don't intend to just read it. I wish to embody it.

She draws a skinny little skeleton with pointy pink nails and messy long red curls and then other skeletons, each with an identifying feature.

"As I enter the assemblage of the walking dead, I wonder who will whisper in my ear during the Intermediate Stage, the State of the Moment of Death?"

Who is she talking to? Should we just assume it is an angel on her shoulder?

The translation she reads indicates it might be a "Brother of Faith" who will whisper in her ear. Because Rachel no longer has a brother. He is dead to her, though still incarnated in a brownstone sitting on the periphery of Prospect Park in Brooklyn, New York.

As she inscribes those who are still alive for her into the *Address Book of the Living* from the *Address Book of the Dead*, she knows nothing on earth will convince her to move his entry from the old book to the new one. He is dead to her. Dead, dead, dead. It is something he engineered himself. And when she was noting that "a new one has died," it was this long-ago lost brother's 89-year-old adopted father who died, this unnatural father of this unnatural brother, not hers, not her father.

Her father died at 31. In the beginning, when God created the sister and brother's heaven and earth, he was both their fathers, this wonderful man who died at 31. Then their mother remarried. The 89-year-old ex-person recently pronounced dead was more like 45 when he beat the boy into submission. And as Vampire Dad, he took him over, made him in his image, made him his son. Vampire Dad just wanted to *make Rachel*, period. She threw up even thinking about it, even now. Even with him dead.

Despite her Jewish upbringing, Rachel is currently drawn to the *Tibetan Book of the Dead*, not to the Torah or even the Bible. This is a new phase for her. She has, as mentioned before, fallen in love with what the Buddhist writings say about coming face-to-face with Clear Light.

Having no "Brother of Faith," or any other brother, she chooses instead a woman she trusts, a "Sister of Faith," to whisper in her ear. The woman is Leonora, a true lioness when it comes to facing the realities of life and then moving on, allowing you to be guided on your course rather than inserting herself and guiding your course for you.

As Rachel recopies names, addresses, and telephone numbers from one address book to the next, she trusts Leonora is there for her. Of course, even in a marriage, *'til death do us part* is tenuous at best. Rachel's mother, Stella, would have been very jealous of Leonora. Leonora is Rachel's therapist.

In her most recent session, Rachel was self-reflective.

"I'm so tired, Leonora. I feel like I'm about to tip over a cliff. Maybe it's this Brooklyn Art Museum project I'm participating in. The Moleskin book must be fifty-one percent writing. The rest can be anything–pictures, collage, a full-page, an empty page–whatever I want. It's due in May and I'm not sure I'm giving it up. It has become my private, fascinating experiment. All-consuming at points. In fact, when I'm done with this therapy session, I've got a page where I pasted a Madame Alexander doll from *Little Women*. Jo, I think. I always wanted one of those dolls and my ex-brother was ready to buy me one at his wife's aunt's store in Cleveland. But his wife stopped him."

Rachel lowered her voice in imitation of her ex-brother's wife and said, "Why do you want to buy a grown woman a doll? Just because she says she wants it? That's ridiculous, Pauly."

Then Rachel screwed up her face as she recalled the scene in the toy store in slow motion. A wide arc of spit came from Dodie's mouth–that was her name, Dodie. "It's disgusting, Paul. My God, she and your mother have certainly trained you well." Which, Rachel realized in the long run, and it was long, was all to Dodie's advantage.

"Go on." Leonora picked up her pad and scribbled a note like therapists are wont to do.

"I wonder if it's writing this notebook, recalling the pain and suffering and loss–and my anger–that tires me."

Leonora, true to her lioness name, has an unruly dark brown head of tendril-like hair that reaches well beyond her shoulders. She has a wonderful habit of tossing her head periodically that beguiles Rachel.

"Of course, dear Rachel, you *are* refashioning the pain and sorrow–remember, it's exhausting to re-live. But that's what your life is right now. And doing all this is exhausting." The wise woman sat back and held eye contact, another trick of the trade, which, by the way, works. The lioness' tresses only emphasized the tall willowy frame which at times looks insubstantial. The thick-rimmed maroon glasses and predilection for dark solid-color clothes help ground Leonora, and this appearance allows her to be taken very seriously by her clients. Rachel takes her very seriously.

"My dreams, my hopes, my fears…" Rachel was crying.

Leonora proffered the floral print tissue box. "Talk about it."

"There is this place in me that was a sore they picked. He, my brother, did it very consciously, viciously. She, my mother, did it with more aplomb by being more passive-aggressive. Plus that ogre who just died in Living-stone, he took the cake, the house, the china, and the silver. He liked to say, 'Rachel, for a smart girl, you're really stupid.' And then he pulled me to him and he stunk. He stunk of those big fat cigars. And he made me kiss him or he wouldn't let go. In any case, to feel better about themselves, all three had to tear me down. To feel powerful, they had to wield power over me. Control me."

"Precisely. And how does that make you feel now?"

"Angry, I guess."

"You guess?"

Rachel smiled half a smile. "Angry! There has to be a cure for this malady of anger and hate and wretched sadness pulling me back into the vortex of this rotten growing-up family core that I no longer live my life up, down, around, and through."

"There is a cure. You're finding your way. You're doing a really good job of it, Rachel. The answer is to keep writing and sketching in your Moleskin book. Keep living." This therapist, a former literature professor, is in sync with Rachel the writer.

"Will the end of this book deliver me from extreme exhaustion, somehow, some way?"

"What do you think?" Leonora the therapist crossed her legs and took a sip of water. "What exactly do *you* think?"

# # #

Rachel was trying to get two items after her mother's funeral, which preceded her stepfather's funeral by three years, two items left in their house. First there was her wedding gown that she requested her mother "heritage" for her, which meant it was preserved and put into a square box in Stella's cedar closet in New Jersey. The second was an oil portrait of Rachel at five, which Rachel wanted to claim possession of, if only to make sure the ex-brother and his family didn't use it for target practice.

It all reminded her about something that happened five years before her mother died. Her mother gave Rachel her baby picture. Little Rachel at six months old. Her mother gave her the original. There was no copy. Why, Rachel wondered. Why wouldn't a mother want to keep a baby picture of her daughter?

At first, Rachel didn't realize it was a mean act. Over time she realized it was just another rejection by her mother of who Rachel was. Maybe in the next life Rachel would get a mother who accepted her unconditionally.

Another reason Rachel liked the *Tibetan Book of the Dead*: It talked about reincarnating. Granted, you only came back to earth rather than ascending, if you had more work to do on yourself here. But Rachel was ready to return and live a happier life. Reincarnation was a process Rachel kept as her dark secret belief, hugged against her 40-D breast. In this one physical way, she did take after her mother.

# # #

A Few Pages from Rachel's Brooklyn Library Moleskin Book: *Leftovers*

[sketch of a plate with parcels of portions left on it—actual sketch here]

We are the ones who are left. We are the leftovers. I, for one, am left on a plate that belonged to my Grandma Bessie. It is her china from Japan. An odd juxtaposition of countries since she was from Russia.

It—the plate—is from the set my mother promised me. Said it was mine and then kept it for herself and bought me off by insisting when I was getting married that he, the thin, sleazy gymnast from Youngstown, Ohio, and I pick out a pattern. So dutiful Richard and dutiful me entered Tiffany's, a ritzy purveyor of unwanted, unneeded wares and picked out a pattern. Pretty with little flowers. But not my grandmother's china. My mother didn't understand the difference and bought us a thousand dollars' worth of this Lenox china at a discount store in Maplewood, New Jersey. We used it twice before the divorce–but we never did use the full twelve place settings. When we stored it in her basement, we forgot it was there. She didn't. Boxes upon boxes. Leftovers just like me. All in all, I'm glad she made me take it home so that it did not go the way of the wedding dress and oil portrait.

Even if it's not the set I wanted. Even if it reminds me that, like the matching crystal goblet my husband broke and said was <u>très chère</u> to replace, my marriage was shattered, laid out in ruins. I guess I'm glad I've got it all–I could always sell it, RIGHT? ["RIGHT" appears in big red capital letters for emphasis.]

OK. Now, that said, mother is dead and ex-brother or "ex-bro," true son of the newly buried 89-year-old, refuses to honor anything she promised me. I must let go of things. Let go of the Victorian oval miniature portrait of a mother and daughter I brought back from my studies in England. Let go of the seven lovely soap hands I sent her when she crowed about how much she adored the one I originally gave her. Let go of her need to be lovelier than me that, by strong inference, made me an ugly duckling.

Perhaps one day I'll unpack the pretty dishes by Lenox. Perhaps I'll put them and their matching crystal, which her dutiful friends bought us along with sterling silver serving pieces, in the dining room. The plates *are* pretty, along with the stemware, just not necessary or practical. Can we look at people like that? Pretty. Not necessary or practical.

I often use my Hadleyware, a whimsical gray and blue set from Louisville, Kentucky with barnyard animals and the farmer and his wife. Sarah-Lynn, my friend from Cleveland and Cuyahoga Community College teaching days, started me collecting. She gifted me with a small round spoon rest, or perhaps it's a teabag holder. Anyway, I was hooked. Hooked on the quaint, non-Jewish type stoneware, not hooked on the mother-driven *nouveau riche* fancy china.

[magazine photo of a formal dining room table set with obviously expensive china, silver, elegant linens and gorgeous expensive flower arrangements replete with lilies, roses, and irises on the left; country kitchen kitsch with an open fireplace, a big oak trestle table set with fanciful Hadleyware, squared-off stainless implements, a bright pink oilcloth table covering, a pottery vase stuffed with wild flowers, replete with baby's breath, daisies, Queen Ann's Lace and cornflowers on

the right]

I am jealous of the other "mother deaths" my friends have shared.

[sketch of mother-body on death bed with room full of people]

Friends such as Mari. The wonderful image of all the people crowding into the beloved woman's room, a woman who was an immigrant sharecropper, a woman who was valued and true to herself and her family. Mari was given the time and grace to squeeze her mother's hand and say "I love you."

[sketch of many hands—hand wallpaper and hand soap]

I had no hand to squeeze that would truly take me in, ever.

I even read a story about a politician and his mother that made me the color of envy. Sherrod Brown, US Senator from Ohio, spent a lot of time away from the Senate–the fucking US Senate, no less–with his mother as she died from Leukemia. I capitalize "Leukemia," grant it power because it *is* such a powerful disease. When asked why he had to be absent from so many votes, Senator Brown told the Senate Majority Leader, Harry Reid, "I only have one mother."

Because he loved his mother and she loved him, he knew his priorities. He needed to be away from the Senate a lot in her final days. From the *Washington Post* description, she sounded like a real treasure. Had her kids call Black people "Mr." and "Mrs." Not by their first names. This was in a past era when they had to sit at the back of the bus and could not be served at "White Only" restaurants. She knew that to call them by their first names was disrespectful. Something my mother and the rest of my family just didn't know. Couldn't look past their own Jewish suffering and martyrdom to recognize it in a dark face.

[photo of Civil Rights anniversary front page Ebony *photograph]*

# # #

Rachel's live-in lover, Jon, puts the worn address book with its golden tree-embossed cover into a baggie. She wanted him to set it out with the recyclables but he had another suggestion. "Let's bury it. If it's the *Tibetan Address Book of the Dead* in your eyes, let's just bury it."

Rachel met Jon 30 years before while tripping in London where she took three summer classes at the University of London, Birbeck, and chased some blotter LSD and soapers down with wine. Briefly they were lovers, remained friends upon returning home, lost track of each other, discovered each other again on Facebook. A modern-day romance story. Jon was a mensch, a decent male human being. Is there an equivalent Yiddish word for a good woman? *Wensch?*

# # #

For red-haired Rachel, there are two kinds of dead in the old address book. The ones she crosses off because they actually stop being in the state we call "alive." Gloria and Liz and Suzanne—mentors, teachers, friends. Asa and Clark—writers, editors, good guys. Aunt Florence and Uncle Howard. Aunt Sandra and Uncle Dave. Jacqueline's dear, dead baby, Nora. Her neighbors' son, Michael, only seven.

Then there are the other kind of dead, dead to Rachel, gone from her life, X-ed off with a big X in the sky.

[picture of big X in cloud-filled O'Keeffe-esque sky]

Those who are dead to Rachel are obvious ones—her brother Paul, his wife Dodie, their daughter and sons; gone, reclaimed by a very busy world that Rachel thanked God every day she didn't fit into. Her dear, dead father's sisters who had actually abandoned her long ago when her mother married the cigar man who just died at 89.

Her paternal aunts: Did they ever call when she was a trapped teen and ask her how she was? Did they ever sit down with her at their homes and try to find out if she was OK—which she wasn't. Hard to believe how much they claim to have loved her father, their brother. Yet they cut off his own flesh and blood. Turning back the pages of her memory, Rachel realizes they were dead to her years ago.

All of them. Now buried with the person she used to call her brother.

# # #

In Rachel's new black-and-white address book, she has new addresses. She has carefully written in names she has not thought of in years. Cousins who have reconnected with her, care about her, are there for her. Good, solid cousins from the beginning of her time on earth. This is good. Life is good. She is entering a period of reuniting through the telephone and Facebook, where she is reconnecting with people from her Livingston High School years. It is all good.

Rachel puts her head down on the glass table. "What's wrong?" Jon asks.

"Oh, life in general can be considered wrong but right now I am choosing to switch that around, make it different. You're a great friend, Jon. To help me in so many ways. Like when they ganged up on me at the funeral and accused me of my mother's death because we hadn't talked in three weeks, but I wrote, I always wrote." This part of the story is always hard for Rachel, always hard. She decides to just focus on today and the book burial and the christening perhaps of the new address book. Yes, that will be better. For today.

So today, in the thin swath of woods behind their rental house, Jon uses a gardening shovel to dig a hole. Rachel removes the old blue address book from the plastic bag and then puts it in the shoebox. "You might want to keep it in that plastic. You never know, Rach, when you might decide you need to 'dig up' one of their addresses or phone numbers."

"Never," she answered. She smoothes her long black skirt worn for the occasion and intones the only appropriate words she can think of: "Ashes to ashes. Dust to dust." She places the Keds shoebox in the hole and cries as Jon hands her a white rose to lay on top of it.

"Ready?"

"Yup. The tears are a mixed bag but I'm ready to bury the past and move on. Of course, the symbolic gesture may be light years ahead of the feelings." Jon looks so sad about what she says as he leans on the shovel. "No. Don't worry, Jon. The healing has begun. Start shoveling that dirty dirt back in the hole.

# # #

A Few Final Pages from Rachel's Brooklyn Library Moleskin Book: *Leftovers*
[picture of clothing left drying and flying over graveyard on clothesline]

Put the black-and-white spiral *Book of the Living* away in an old desk whose drawer bottom has fallen out many times. I look out my second-floor window and am protected from the snow curtain that blows toward me. Protected by a many-paned window, protected by care and love. The trees look even more beautiful, if that is possible, with their soft goose down coverings outlining their branches, outlining the pine needles, outlining the outside life. I am inside and watch the wind's trajectory change.

I have lit incense from Mother Meera and chosen an Oracle card: Enchantment. A card reminding me to believe in the joy of life that so many leave behind in childhood. I left it behind earlier than that. I wish to reclaim it. This book is a reclamation project.

If I narrow my gaze, I can see where we buried the *Tibetan Address Book of the Dead*. I watch as bamboo and weeds take over the small empty burial plot. The truth is, I've buried each and every one of them in my heart. Like all decomposition, these painful memories of people who "done me wrong" will drift into nothingness, become meaningless blips on my computer screen, become a short story.

LITTLE MISS SASSY

Little Miss Sassy
sat in a grassy
field eating brains and whey.
There came a great spider,
put venom inside her,
and murdered Miss Sassy,
hurrah!

THE CROOKED SPIRIT

There was a crooked spirit
not Father, Son, or Host.
He found himself a crooked soul
and made of him a ghost.
He took a crooked match
and lit a funeral pyre.
Then slowly roasted flesh and bone
over the crooked fire.

SKIN SUIT

David Yurkovich

A FIGHT ERUPTED THIS MORNING in the third floor recreation room. Nothing serious. Just the usual skirmish that occurs when one resident discovers that another resident has something (in this instance, a birthday card) that he lacks. So it was that fifty-three-year-old Robert Wallace attacked the slightly younger Josh McMillan, landing a few choice blows before the orderlies removed him from the room. Josh was fine of course–a tough exterior and interior. Not sure why he's here because, truth is, he seems completely rational. Never seen him lost in conversation with imaginary people (or invisibles, as the staff around here call them), has never acted irrational, never threatened a soul. Far as I can tell, Josh is completely and utterly sane.

No one visits me here. Been that way for years. Truth is, I shouldn't be here at all. I was guilty and should have gone to state prison. Not that I minded the sentence. A skinny white man with red hair, freckles, and glasses wouldn't have done well in state. My state-appointed public defender figured that much and struck an agreement with the prosecution, much to the lament of the deceased's family and the local press.

It's worked out okay. I don't mind this place on most days, though I do miss C.F. I also miss Shelley. Seems like forever since we last spoke, and probably it has, though I don't much watch the clock, much less the calendar.

You've read about me. I was born in suburban Detroit on June 13, 1930, and christened Bridger, the only child of Lloyd and Mildred Reiterman. My mother worked as a seamstress. Dad owned a small but profitable butcher shop. Our family was solvent even through the worst of the Great Depression. Mom and dad worked seven days a week in shifts of 12 hours to make ends meet. Following the attack on the Pearl Harbor Navy Base on December 7, 1941, by the Imperial Japanese Navy, dad, like so many others, enlisted in the US Army. I was eleven and given the responsibility of managing the butcher shop in his absence. A tall order for sure, but I had been around the business since I was four years old. By age seven I already knew how to quarter a carcass and use a meat saw, knew how to cure and how to grind. I did okay.

Three years later, on December 31, 1944, mom got notice that dad had been among the 3,000 soldiers killed in Operation North Wind in northwestern Europe. Shortly after the war ended, she moved us to western Pennsylvania. For a while, we lived with relatives before renting a small apartment in North Fairmont. I found work with a local butcher for several years, but had no interest in setting up my own business. Folks say I seldom smiled. Seems like there was little to smile about.

Every town has its bully. In North Fairmont his name was Barton Garrison. He was a big kid with ham-like arms. Everyone feared Garrison. He enjoyed taunting me, and I took it all in stride until an afternoon in March of 1945 when Garrison beat me. It happened on the walk home from school. Knocked me down, took off his belt and wrapped it around the fingers of his right hand, and landed more blows than I could count. I still remember him standing there, so proud of his achievement.

"We're gonna do this every day," he said. "Every day."

The following afternoon, I walked over to his house on Kaymer Street. Barton was standing by the side of the house lighting up a smoke.

"Back for more?" he asked, tossing the cigarette to the ground.

I moved swiftly, the granton-edge steel emerging suddenly from my back pocket. It was a short boning knife I'd pilfered from the butcher's store. Four-inch blade. I tore into Garrison as if he were cattle, and his white fitted t-shirt turned spotty crimson. Garrison fell to the ground, palms pressed against open wounds. So many beautiful open wounds.

"I need more hands," he winced, unable to stop the bleeding.

"Don't be stupid," I said, and dropped onto his back.

"You touch me, or anyone else ever again, we're gonna do this every day. Every day."

Garrison was crying and gagging and he started to piss his pants. I pressed the blade tight against his neck and drew blood.

"We clear, Bart?"

He nodded, body trembling.

I graduated school in June 1948 and found work with the US Postal Service as a letter carrier. I'd sprouted during adolescence and was nearly six feet tall though all of 110 pounds. Some of the crew referred to me as "Golden Gate." Most, however, simply avoided me, as I'd become known as the freak butcher boy with a quick temper. Not that it mattered; I disliked people about as much as I liked the outdoors and walking. Year after year, the summer sun tanned my fair, freckled skin.

In 1953 everything changed.

Felix Brunswell of 117 Charming Road was one of the hundreds of residents on my route. He was an older fellow who had recently moved into the neighborhood. One afternoon is June, he stepped out of his house, ran down the sidewalk, and began accursing me of stealing his mail. I tried to shrug it off, but then he struck me on the shoulder with a walking stick. Even then, I tried to walk away, but Brunswell just kept on hitting me.

Finally I hit back. Smashed the upper lateral cartilage of Brunswell's nose. Lost my route and was transferred to an indoor job, serving as the lone postal clerk for a rural office in Hamptonshire (population 903), ten miles east of North Fairmont. I also had to meet with a psychiatrist to talk about my feelings of anger. I endured several sessions with Sebastian Connor, a strict Freudian.

"Your anger issues are the result of feelings within your unconscious mind permeating his consciousness," he babbled.

"Why am I angry?" I played along.

"You are, in my estimation," he said, "using anger as a means of self-soothing."

"Self-soothing?"

"You have had loss in your life, Bridger. In a scant 23 years, you've lost your father, your home, and friends. You have been bullied. And you now have been relegated from a position within the postal service that offered you freedom of movement to a stationary desk job–a mere clerk. In a sense you've lost all autonomy."

"Jesus. When you put it that way I feel like I should find the nearest noose."

"You're incorporating anger as a means of survival. If left unchecked, you will certainly self-destruct."

"What can I do?"

"Have you heard of iproniazid?"

And just like that, I began taking antidepressants.

The postal job was fine. I sorted the mail and placed letters into post office boxes. The mail to be delivered to residents curb side was picked up each morning by Coleman Francis, a veteran of the USPS who had recently gone into semi-retirement. Aside from the morning pick-ups and drop-offs, I never saw much of Coleman.

I met C.F. Hoffmeyer a short time later, in August 1953. I admit that I was immediately impressed by him. An eclectic fellow of 29 years, C.F. was the only Hamptonshire resident who, as far as I knew, collected postage stamps.

"You're new. What happened to Penske?" he asked.

"Penske relocated to Miami."

"Miami? How dreadful. Though I'm sure the weather is nicer. I simply cannot abide Pennsylvania in August. I presume you have full sheets of Scott 1022 for sale?"

"Scott 1022?"

"Yes, the American Bar Association three-cent issue, released last week."

"Ah, yes. Of course."

"I'll take five sheets."

I retrieved the sheets from a drawer and watched as C.F. eyed them with the strictest scrutiny. A short, stout fellow with bifocal eyeglasses, thick black locks, and an olive complexion, I soon discovered that C.F. was keen on sharing his knowledge of the philatelic world. In little time he expanded my own stamp knowledge ten-fold, though I didn't embrace the hobby much more than casually. Nonetheless, C.F. and I became fast, inseparable friends. Ever adorned in a vest and pleated trousers, he was well educated and self-employed as a corporate law consultant, with clients located as far south as Pittsburgh.

While in Hoffmeyer's third-story apartment we transitioned from friends to lovers. It happened on June 18, 1956, rather unintentionally as these things sometimes do. Until that moment, I had never actually considered my sexuality nor thought about a relationship with either gender, but was awestruck by Hoffmeyer's advances. As I later explained to my public defender, I never labeled myself as hetero- or homosexual; my willingness to enter into a relationship with C.F. was something that just felt right.

Shelley Arnquest entered my life later that same year. A well-dressed petite woman of twenty-four, Shelley visited the Hamptonshire Post Office on random Mondays, always at 10:13 AM. Her attire never varied: black dress with matching pointed-toe pumps and sequin purse. Her skin was fair and her shoulder-length hair, auburn. I noticed the presence of dimples even when she wasn't smiling. Shelley typically purchased one- or five-cent stamps. We chatted frequently, and Shelley was often quick to offer a bit of nondescript unsolicited advice about the weather or relationships. Often she spoke in riddles; truthfully, I regarded her as a peculiarity.

C.F. and I remained understandably clandestine in our affair. Hamptonshire and North Fairmont were largely comprised of white conservatives with an ideology that eschewed nonconformity to longstanding traditional moral values. We understood this all too well, having personally witnessed the thrashing of an out-of-town samesex male couple several months earlier outside the Hamptonshire VFW.

In the fall of 1956, as the IBM Corporation was releasing the first computer to contain a built-in hard drive, we settled into a comfortable familiarity. C.F. gave me a key to his flat. I still lived at my mom's North Fairmont home, where C.F. and I spent many hours, particularly in the early evenings as mom had transitioned from seamstress to switchboard operator working the 4:00 PM to midnight shift at the Bell offices in nearby Hartsdell.

On January 5, 1957, while updating the FBI's Most Wanted flyers pinned to the lobby corkboard, I was visited by Shelley, who had not been by for several weeks.

"Good morning, Bridger, and Happy New Year."

"Good morning to you. Shelley, do you think it strange that post offices are required to hang posters–missing persons, most wanted?"

"Lots of people visit post offices. And lots of people go missing. Lots."

"I suppose. Are you here for stamps?"

"We need to talk."

"Is something wrong?"

"Something is very wrong–well, is going to be wrong," Shelley said, her usual cat-and-mouse tone turning serious. "What do you know about this town, about Hamptonshire?"

"What's there to know?"

"Every town has its history, Bridger. Small towns like this, their histories are often rooted in the unnatural or the supernatural."

"Supernatural."

"Hamptonshire has a past. A bad past; you're too young to know about it."

"We're practically the same age."

Shelley frowned.

"Your presence here is going to ignite a spark long since dormant."

"Could you be a little more cryptic?"

"I've said too much already."

She looked over her shoulder, detecting a shadow, but it was only the sun disappearing into the clouds.

"Are you okay, Shelley?"

"Ask about Dereleth Abercrombie. Or Elizabeth Wilkinson."

She left abruptly.

"Oh yes, there was quite a mystery over those two," C.F. said later that evening as he sipped Merlot from a long-stemmed glass.

"What happened?"

"It's all folklore and superstition, of course, neither of which I subscribe to. But since you're asking, your curiosity I shall attempt to satiate. In September of 1910 the little town of Hamptonshire experienced its first-ever murder. Dereleth Abercrombie was a coachman at the time and was found with his throat slit on Mulberry Street in mid-October of that year. He'd been drained of all blood. There was no other apparent robbery; no obvious reason for the crime. Some years later, Elizabeth Wilkinson, who worked as a dress maker on Reed Street, was also killed in a similar fashion. The assailant or assailants were never found."

"Horrific, but hardly supernatural."

"Except . . ."

"Except?"

"Some claim to have seen Abercrombie and Wilkinson since then."

"Ghost sightings?"

"Ghosts. Spirits. The undead. Whatever label you'd like to put on it."

"You're suggesting that the dead haunt Hamptonshire?"

"I'm suggesting no such thing. I'm only stating that, in the years since the murders occurred, both victims have been spotted in town on multiple occasions."

"Still don't know how any of it relates to me," I said.

"Probably it doesn't," C.F. said, filling both our glasses.

The following evening, as C.F. and I walked toward the Smith Saloon, I stopped suddenly and, pointing at my mouth, asked, "What is this . . .thing . . .that I'm feeling?"

"I believe it's called happy," C.F. replied.

I clutched C.F.'s gloved hand, realizing at that moment that I had in fact found contentment.

The Hamptonshire Tavern held the usual Friday night regulars, tallying less than one dozen in number, and the nickel drafts flowed freely. Jimmy Wise, who ran a small auto-repair shop and was known to all as The Wise Man, sat at his usual corner stool, a trail of smoke from the tip of a cigarette rising listlessly from ashtray to air. Ingrid and Joshua Sawyer, owners of Hamptonshire Dairy and Produce (the only game in town for groceries) stood chatting with barkeep Mick Hendrickson about an approaching snowstorm. The remaining locals, Huntz Myrtle among them, bickered heatedly over the future of the Pittsburgh Pirates under the management of Bobby Bragan and absentmindedly shot pool. C.F and I entered without fanfare and approached the bar. Shortly after 11:00 PM, we entered the men's room and vanished behind the door of its only stall, returning to our bar seats fifteen minutes later.

Shelley visited me again on January 14.

"You really like that dress," I said.

"Yes, I suppose I do."

"I looked into Dereleth Abercrombie and Elizabeth Wilkinson like you suggested. But I don't believe in ghosts and I don't see how either of their deaths relates to me."

"I might not believe that an airplane can fly across the ocean, but that doesn't make it any less true," Shelley countered.

"Airplanes are tangible machines, built with steel and aluminum by engineers. Ghosts are little more than the workings of the imagination, the stuff of Poe and Lovecraft."

"Dereleth and Elizabeth's spirits haunt Hamptonshire; you can be certain of this. It's been said that the earth here is cursed, and sometimes, well, sometimes the dead refuse to stay dead."

"That makes no sense at all."

"You'll find, Bridger, that not everything makes sense. Does it make sense that your dad was killed in 1944 during the war? Does it make sense that you were taunted in school by Barton Garrison? Does it make sense that secrets about our relationships must be kept in order to maintain personal safety?

"Have you been spying on me?" I asked.

"I'd like five stamps please," she said, retrieving a quarter from her purse.

"How do you know so much about me, Shelley?"

"Stamps please," she repeated, and placed the coin on the counter.

"Answer the goddam question!" I demanded.

"You wouldn't believe me if I told you. So why don't I show you instead?"

She reached into her handbag and retrieved a small sheet of paper, an old newspaper clipping, folded over several times and handed it to me. I unfolded the paper. After a minute or so, I slid it back across the countertop toward Shelley.

"You're telling me that this newspaper article is about you. That you went missing in February of 1926 on your twenty-fourth birthday?"

"Bridger, I was strangled and died in February of 1926 on my twenty-fourth birthday."

I noticed, for the first time, the thin line of discoloration around her neck, a line no wider than a shoelace or telephone cord.

"I think the article's a fake. I think you're a liar and a fraud."

"More proof then?"

Shelly began to press the fingers of her right hand against her dress and slightly to the left of the breastbone. Her fingers melted through the dress and into her flesh. She pulled her heart through her rib cage with a loud cracking sound and held it before me. The organ was dry and decayed, the arteries long since desiccated. The right atrium was mud brown and fully collapsed. I stumbled back and fell to the ground, crawling in reverse like a frightened child.

A moment later she was kneeling next to me. I screamed and shut my eyes tight.

"What do you want? What do you want?" I whispered.

"I'm not here to frighten you, to haunt you. My soul is restless, has been restless for nearly forty years when my life was taken away at 10:13 on my twenty-fourth birthday. I'm only here to help you. Soon you'll be faced with choices, and the choice you make will have lifelong ramifications. Just be sure . . . be sure to make good choices."

"Go away, Shelley. I don't want your help. Just go away."

Shelley silently walked toward the cash register and retrieved her postage stamps before stepping through the counter itself and through the door. Following a few hasty swallows of spiced rum from a flask tucked away in my desk, I began to contemplate that Shelley did not actually exist. She was, I realized, a spirit not of the grave but of my own making. Upon further introspection I concluded that the Shelley persona was merely a manifestation of my subconscious mind. Another means of self-soothing, as my psychiatrist had deemed it. I realized that this theory was not without its problems, but it would suffice until I could think upon it further. In the interim, I decided that rather than reject Shelley's future appearances, I would welcome them, in hopes of revealing their true purpose, one that I was certain transcended ghosts and goblins. In the ensuing weeks I did not see Shelley; however, I did not mind her absence from my life.

There were many things Charlie Attenborough might have

done on March 29. For example, he could have taken the day off from work and rested his ailing hip. He could have phoned his aged Mother, Delores, a resident of the Sunnyside Retirement Home, just to issue a long overdue hello. He could have dropped off a back-rent check with his landlord, Sammy Watersmith. Lots of things. Instead, Charlie Attenborough visited the post office.

Charlie arrived just prior to the 5:00 PM closing. I watched though the glass panel of the front door as he sucked in the brisk afternoon air and stepped out of his maroon Chevy. Attenborough was a stocky, balding man who worked as a contract electrician. His hands were heavily calloused and he was prone to sudden outbreaks of psoriasis.

"Gotta grab the mail," he said, pushing open the door and waving a key near my face as I attempted to lock up.

"No problem."

He opened and closed his post office box.

"Typical; nothing but bills," he said, slipping the envelopes into his front pocket.

"How's it going, Bridger?"

"Going okay, I guess."

He cut right to the chase. "You, uh, dating anyone these days? Special lady friend maybe?"

I started at Attenborough and shook my head slightly.

"No. I didn't think so. See, the thing is, I seen you. Month or two back. You and Hoffmeyer. I seen you in the men's room at the tavern. Seen and heard. That ain't right. What you're doing ain't natural," Charlie said, shaking his head in exaggerated disapproval.

"Of course, it's none of my business what a man—what two men—do with their personal lives. But, ya know, information like that in the wrong hands. Fellow could get hurt, or worse. Much worse."

"What do you want, Charlie?" I asked, discretely and quietly inserted a key into the inside cylinder housing of the door lock before rotating it clockwise.

What followed was a brief tête-à-tête during which time a verbal agreement was reached.

"You're a smart man, Bridger. And I'll expect the first installment by the end of this week."

"I'm glad we've reached a consensus," I nodded and extended a hand as Charlie approached the locked door. There was no handshake. The blade concealed between my index and middle finger was miniscule, a little penknife I kept in my pocket and used on envelopes and packages. I closed my hand into a fist and quickly drove the blade upward into Attenborough's pudgy neck, smashing his windpipe while tearing through flesh. Charlie reeled and fell backward and against the wall of metal mailboxes as a light spray of blood splashed side to side and decorated the room in a primal crimson graffiti.

Later that evening, I returned to the building with C.F., who followed me through the lobby and past the cashier area of the building. We stepped through a door and walked toward a small room where mail was typically sorted. The darkness through which we moved was broken only by a metal flashlight. C.F. shook his head in disbelief.

"Christ. What a mess. You could have simply agreed to pay him, old chap," C.F. said, staring at the corpse sprawled out along the floor.

"What's done is done," I whispered.

"I suppose so. What's the game plan? Do you have one?" C.F. asked.

"I do."

I retrieved and unlatched a black tackle box from an adjacent desk. The metal blades within glistened against the glow of the flashlight and I passed a cleaver to C.F.

"Jesus Christ, Bridger. Is this really necessary? I mean, he's dead, right?"

"He is. I just want to make certain he stays that way."

Prior to the dismemberment, C.F. and I affixed rope around Attenborough's body and tossed the slack over an exposed ceiling beam. We hefted the corpse into the air and knotted the rope. The body hung suspended several feet above ground like a dead cow. I grabbed a pair of sewing scissors and began cutting through Attenborough's clothing. Next, I removed his sneakers and slipped on a pair of rubber knee boots before snagging a butcher's apron and fastening it securely around my waist. Lastly, I draped a plastic tarp across the floor and placed a utility bucket over the tarp.

"First things first," I said, and made a small incision into Attenborough's anterior jugular vein. A thin trickle of blood emerged, spiralling downward and into the awaiting bucket. C.F. gasped.

MILTON WORKSHOP ANTHOLOGY SERIES

"This is going to take a few minutes. Why don't you help out by cleaning up the mess in the lobby? There are towels and soap, and a bucket, in the closet."

"Sure. I'm on it," C.F. said. I could see that he was relieved to distance himself from the carnage that was soon to follow.

Two things about butchering, that is, the act of dissecting a dead thing for the purposes of consumption: First, once you've acquired the skill, you don't really lose it. I hadn't held the tools of the trade for some time, but it all came back quickly as though it had never gone away. The second thing—and this was something I was about to discover—is that from a dismemberment perspective, there's little difference between animal and man. I knew that the removal of the large and small intestines would be the most gruesome aspect of the task ahead and quickly set to work. The stomach, colons, rectum, and liver were easily dislodged with an eight-inch scimitar knife and placed in a second utility bucket. A standard cleaver sufficed for the remainder of the job. Twenty-four sections in all, neatly arranged across the blue tarp long before C.F. had completed his negligible janitorial task.

Upon seeing the body is this new state, C.F. made a hasty retreat to the restroom and vomited, returning minutes later.

"Sorry about that," he said. "It's just, well, what now?"

I gazed around the shadowed room at the various boxes, package tape, and other mail provisions at our disposal.

Ultimately we nixed my idea of shipping the body parts to random PO boxes across the globe and instead buried the sections in the wooded area behind the Hamptonshire Post Office. It was exhausting work—the earth was cold but, thankfully not frozen—and we completed the grim task before dawn. The intestines—bucket and all—were dumped into nearby Joiner's Creek and quickly sank.

"That's everything," C.F. said, wiping sweat from his brow.

"Yep."

We returned to the post office, removing any additional faint traces of blood or guts from the premises. I cleaned my blades and returned them to the tackle box and then walked toward the sorting table while carrying package tape and a long strip of plastic. Moments later I carted Attenborough's skull across the floor toward the office safe. I opened the safe, pushed aside a cash register drawer, and placed the skull inside before quickly shutting the door and rotating the combination.

"What the fuck are you thinking?" C.F. said.

"I'll deal with the head tomorrow, maybe grind it to powder. Until then, it stays locked in the safe, out of harm's way."

"You really think that's necessary?"

"The dead will not be coming back," I said, turning suddenly and grasping C.F.'s arms tightly."

"You're losing it, Bridger. For Christ's sake, you're a murderer. You killed a man!"

"I'll do it again if I have to! And again after that. I won't allow our lives to be jeopardized by working class homophobes, and neither should you."

"I'm sorry," C.F. said, backing away. "Just . . . just get rid of the head, okay? No good can come of keeping it around."

"I already told you I'd deal with it. Listen to me. It'll be light soon. We need to move his truck. Park it back in his driveway, then lock its doors and throw away the keys."

"Okay. Okay, sure."

We returned to C.F.'s flat just before sunrise. I showered and dressed in fresh clothing. C.F. showered and, exhausted, fell quickly asleep. I made toast a coffee but had no appetite, so I returned to the post office to begin the work day.

There was no foul smell lingering in the air. No hint of death or blood. Only the chemical smell of cleaning agents. Feeling a renewed sense of security, I switched on the lights and waited for Coleman to arrive with the morning mail delivery. I felt a sudden closeness to C.F. that transcended the physical intimacy of our relationship. He'd seen me at my most savage and had not turned away but had instead descended into the mire with me. I walked toward the back of the office and waved a hand at the dozen odd gnats in my path. I then retrieved a can of Eight O'Clock Coffee from the cupboard and removed the lid from the percolator.

At 10:13 AM while sorting the mail I was visited by Shelley Arnquest, adorned in her usual black garb. We didn't speak for several awkward moments.

"What do you want, Shelley?" I asked.

"A handful of the one-cent issues. Five, if you have them."

"I'm all out of the penny stamps. Matter of fact, I don't have any stamps to sell to you."

"What's wrong?"

"You know, I was ready to believe that you're just a figment of my imagination. Maybe some sort of ethereal consciousness that would steer me along the right path. But if that's true, why didn't you prevent me from . . ."

"From what?" she asked.

"Nothing. Never mind."

"Have you ever taken anything that wasn't yours to take?" Shelley asked.

"I don't really feel like talking to you."

Undeterred, Shelley stood and stared until I responded.

"You mean like shoplifting?" I asked.

"Not exactly."

"Well . . . probably. I'm not sure."

"It's not healthy to hold onto things that we're not meant to keep."

"I'll try to keep that in mind."

"On another topic, I think you should leave early today."

"Why?"

"Storm coming. If you don't leave soon, you may never make it home."

"The skies are clear, Shelley. The sun is shining."

"I have a riddle for you, Bridger: How are weather forecasts and people both alike?"

"I'm sure I don't know," I said flatly, too tired for brainteasers from beyond the grave.

"Both can change without warning, with terrible outcomes."

"I'll try to remember that. If you don't mind, I'm kind of busy here," I said.

Shelley departed and I returned to mail sorting, finding concentration difficult. It wasn't until mid-afternoon that I noticed the ice storm in progress. Long, jagged icicles hung from the power lines like paper cutouts. I considered heeding Shelley's advice, but the ice was already an inch thick and the storm showed no signs of slowing. Still, I tried to walk to C.F.'s flat, but fell a half-dozen times in the post office parking lot and made a hasty retreat. Ice turned to heavy snow, and by 3:00 PM over six inches of powder covered the ground.

It wasn't the first time I'd bunked in the post office and I figured that it likely wouldn't be the last. As darkness fell, I grabbed a pillow and sleeping bag I kept stashed in the closet and switched on a transistor radio. An announcer on KB15 was highlighting news of the Eisenhower Doctrine, but the details were lost to heavy static. I snagged a half-empty bottle of Bordeaux and drunk deep. I grabbed the receiver of the phone and was in mid-dial when the power failed. From the window I spied several downed cables, toppled, I suppose, by the weight of the snow and ice. I attempted the phone call again but there was no dial tone. A few minutes later I dropped to the floor, slid into the sleeping bag, and finished the wine. Sleep quickly arrived.

I awoke before dawn, stiff neck pain interrupting my sleep. The room was cold. I walked to the windows that overlooked Jacobs Street, aware of a municipal snow plow that crawled along clearing the blocked roadway. So much for Shelley's forboding warning. The electric and phone were still out. I quickly laced up my shoes and grabbed my jacket.

I walked past the office safe and closed its door, nearly slipping on dry patches of dirt atop an otherwise polished linoleum floor. The short walk to the car was still treacherous and I fell a half dozen times before sliding into the front seat. The cold steering wheel upon my fingertips jarred me further awake.

The drive to C.F.'s flat was slow but doable. I entered the darkened dwelling and quietly closed the door before undressing and sliding into bed next to my sleeping lover.

The morning sun, an unwelcome intruder, awoke me from my sleep. I began to draw soft invisible lines upon C.F.'s back with my right index finger. C.F. breathed lightly. I pressed my fingers along C.F.s neck and ran them slowly down his spine.

Something wasn't right. I felt the outline of a laceration where I knew there should be none.

"Did you injure yourself?" I whispered.

I felt a sticky moistness as my fingers descended toward C.F.'s lumbar spine, and I realized suddenly that the gash spanned the full length of his back. I pushed away and scrambled out of the bed in search of the light switch, but the power was still out. C.F. turned ever so slowly. His face appeared twisted and stretched out. I stumbled further away from the bed and tripped over a bulky object in the middle of the floor. A naked body. Cold, wet. So wet. I realized that its skin had been completely removed as if it was a jumpsuit. But there was no doubting the shape and size.

There was no time to ponder the how or why of it. The corpse of Charlie Attenborough staggered out of the bed toward me, its severed limbs somehow reformed and nestled snugly within the skin, the skin suit, of my beloved C.F. I screamed, stumbling backward toward the kitchen. The horror lumbered toward me slowly, mouth agape. The grotesquerie continued to stagger ahead, right hand extended and index finger pointing accusingly. I felt around the kitchen countertop, my hands coming to rest upon a cutting knife.

Terror and fear dissolved into composure and self-assurance.

I awoke hours later, seated in the back seat of a police cruiser, hands cuffed and eyes shut tight. I exhaled deeply and opened my eyes at the sound of a familiar voice.

"I'm sorry it's ending this way for you," Shelley said.

"How did you get in here? Never mind, I know how you got in here. Can anyone else see you?"

"Not really. Death isn't the end, you know. It's just a stage in a longer journey."

"Why did you choose to haunt me?"

"I tried to help you."

"You did a terrific job. I've lost mind, haven't I?"

"I don't think you've lost your mind."

"Maybe I never had one to lose. What's to become of me?"

"I'm a spirit, not a fortune teller. I'm going to miss visiting with you at the post office."

"Why did Attenborough kill C.F.? Why didn't he simply kill me while I slept?"

"I'm sorry. I don't have all the answers."

"Will I ever see you again?"

I waited for Shelley to reply, but quickly realized that she was no longer there.

In every story it seems there are two sides, sometimes more. And even though Hamptonshire has a reputation as being haunted, if not cursed, no one believed my tale. The prosecution, as well as the defense, connected the dots in the easiest way possible: After killing and dismembering Charlie Attenborough, I suffered a total mental collapse. Distraught with guilt, I collected Charlie's body parts and attempted to reassemble them using the skin of C.F. Hoffmeyer. (Allegedly I felt guilt and shame over my physical relationship with C.F. and, therefore, felt justified in his killing.)

There was no tolerance for talk of ghosts or reanimated corpses in a public courtroom, and my testimonies were largely dismissed and treated as further proof of my compromised mentality. The news clipping about Shelley's disappearance in February 1926 was regarded as evidence that the entire affair had been fashioned from within my mind, or, as the prosecution stated it: "Yes, people do go missing. No, they do not subsequently appear as ghosts to haunt random postal clerks."

In the years since my sentencing, I've long since learned to accept the hand I've been given, having in many ways been my own dealer. Most nights I sleep well enough. Not well, but well enough. And though it's always just a pillow to which I'm clinging, on some mornings I wake up, fully convinced that C.F. and I are snuggled tight next to each other. Though the ghosts of the past may fade over time, they seldom die.

LITTLE JACK CORONER

Little Jack Coroner
sat dead in a corner
while I made my
Christmas pie.
I stuck in my thumb
and pulled out his tongue
and said, "Oh such a good baker
am I!"

THE TRUCK

Dianne Pearce

NO ONE EXPECTED HIM TO win the election when he brazenly announced his candidacy at the start of primary season. He was a joke: a terrible businessman and a TV flop who wore obviously fake hair. That you could buy products bearing his name in the dollar stores did not make him a success. He would do nothing but waste his own money.

Millie and her husband and daughter carried on covering their lawn with liberal primary signage. When they had their weekly pot-luck dinners with their other similarly liberal friends, or walked together with their set to the local brewery to sample the newest seasonal brew, they discussed the odds of success for the more reasonable right-wing candidates, but never him. As they passed the kale salad around the large and filled kitchen table, or took their seats on the curb of the brewery, slowly sipping their cold craft pints from BPA-free plastic cups while the kids climbed in and out of the wagons they had pulled them in, they worried en masse about the chicken farmer turned senator from Missouri who had decided to run, or the anti-gay evangelical from Iowa who was throwing his hat into the ring as well. The man from the TV show never entered the conversation in any serious way.

Until he became the conversation.

He held a rally in South-Bumfuck-Somewhere-Or-Other, and as he was speaking, someone heckled him. A man in the small crowd pushed the heckler. The Candidate didn't miss a beat. "Punch him and I'll pay your legal fees!" ripped through the air from the microphone. Six people threw themselves onto the heckler, who was later hospitalized with two cracked ribs, a broken jaw, a concussion, and every finger snapped.

The Candidate went from joke to run-away train in that instant. He mowed the other conservative candidates down with ease, and left the liberals spinning in their shoes, confused and disoriented at his mass appeal.

If the election cycle was a shock to Millie and her family and friends, post-inauguration was worse. The Candidate, who Millie now referred to as The Occupant, did not simmer down once he had the circular office around him, and the much-coveted chair under his ass. He continued to whip-up the crowds on whatever topic the loud and poorly educated called for.

Immigrants? They stole your jobs. Throw 'em out; beat 'em up; I'll pay your legal fees.

Gays and lesbians? They want to touch your children. Knock them down, kick them out of their jobs and apartments; I'll pay your legal fees.

Jews? Blacks? Muslims? Deface the cemeteries, burn the churches, rip off the headscarves; I'll pay your legal fees.

The newspapers, thankfully, fought back. Investigative journalists investigated as if their very lives depended on it. They took down the Chief of Staff, the head of the FBI, the Secretary of Education. Millie was so proud of them. She used photos of them as her profile photo, and so did her friends.

The war between the do-gooders and The Occupant's disciples raged back and forth on TV and in social media: a riot here, a cabinet member exposed there . . .

And then, in just three days, the gloves on both sides came off.

Day 1: A very respected old newspaper ran video on its new-fangled website of The Running Mate soliciting sex from a thirteen-year-old-boy in a Mall of America bathroom. He had offered the boy, a slight but mighty undercover cop in disguise, a new iPhone for a blow job with a finger up the bum.

Day 2: A gang of white supremacists driving a black passenger van covered in swastikas mowed through a crowd marching for illegal immigrants in Berkeley. Though many were injured, no one was killed, which the white supremacists claimed was a merciful warning to all.

Day 3: In an attempt to minimize what he viewed as his running mate's unfair trouble with the law, The Occupant declared war on a small and impotent nation in some sea near Asia or somewhere, and with that, he had wartime powers. He shut down all TV stations, all cable companies, and he locked the doors on all printing presses in the nation, except those that printed the rags that favored him. The internet he left open, simply because he was addicted to texting, but all phone service was limited to video and text messaging until further notice. When the phone monopolies howled, he slipped them disaster relief to shut them up.

At first, though they shook their heads as they sipped their beer, Mille and her crew didn't worry. It seemed that most of the damage was in the super-liberal northwest, and they were in the northeast, and all were sure this blatant abuse of powers would cause even the most divided Congress to act as one. The days of beer and potlucks continued; school continued; their jobs continued; and faith in their system of government remained strong.

Then one day, as they met under an October sky which was hazy and slightly damp under the soft mist of steam issuing from the hops boiling in the kettles somewhere inside the brewery, the bartender yelled out, "He's missing!"

Twenty-six phones emerged from twenty-six pockets and simultaneously hit Google like an information flash mob.

The words winked up at them from *The Post, The Journal,* and even *The Nationalist.* The Occupant had disappeared. He had last texted the morning before. And then he had strode out masterfully to one of his carts and ridden forth over one of his eponymous golf courses, as he did most days while running the country. Security detail patrolled the perimeter of all his golf courses, but none were allowed to sully the green with their working-man's shoes, and so his games remained private. On this particular day, halfway through the course, he'd sent his secretary back to the clubhouse for drinks. Then his caddy went to "help" a ball that he had hit into the rough make it to the green. When the caddy failed to return after a few minutes, he'd instructed his golf buddy, the CEO of Shale Oil, to go help. None of them were away from The Occupant for long, but when the secretary, caddy, and CEO met back up at the two golf carts, the carts were still there, but not the man in charge. He was gone. They waited dutifully until it began to rain, at which point the secretary threw the drinks-tray onto the green and insisted they return to the club to alert security.

The Post called it a hoax for publicity. *The Journal* called it a disturbing twist in The Nation's unrest. *The Nationalist* called it a German conspiracy because The Occupant had made a fat joke about the chancellor in one of his texts. The white-supremacy groups called it their moment, and they struck out with fury, vandalizing anything in their path that represented an alternative to their world view: universities, synagogues, discos, immigration offices.

Still the northeast seemed untouched by it all. As the stories flowed from various news apps over the following weeks it became clear that The Running Mate had had a long and loosely hidden trail of young boys in his past, due in large part to the homosexual-conversion ministry he ran. And so just as The Occupant went missing, The Running Mate was standing before a judge posting bail. No one seemed to know who should be in command even though there was a clearly delineated rule for succession in The Constitution, and they could have easily Googled the information.

After a few weeks with no leader stepping in to quell the daily attacks dished-out by hate groups, tales of a new terror appeared in whispers on Facebook.

At first the descriptions were lacking. People claimed to happen upon heaps of dead bodies, but not to know what caused them to be dead. It was confirmed by several reputable news websites that, yes, horribly enough, there were indeed large numbers of dead, but the cause of death was still unknown. If the bodies were warm when found, the first-responders usually became gravely ill as well, and a few perished. If the corpses were cold, everyone who came in contact with them seemed to stay healthy. And no matter how secret or spontaneous a gathering for the left was, death found it expeditiously, before one step in protest could be taken.

Millie and her crew had theories. The Occupant's disappearance was a stunt. He was not dead, or missing. And he was, in fact, through his control of everything under his wartime powers, torturing good liberals and peace activists to find out their plans, and then forcing the victim to return to the group with cookies laced with cyanide, or mysterious poster paint that leached into the skin and caused instant death. In a way, so aware of what was going on, but so far from the fray as they were, Millie and all her friends felt protected under the changing autumn leaves, as if discussing the mysterious new deaths was not different from the post-game talk after binge-watching the latest Netflix craze.

It was Gerald Xavier Dongle who discovered the truth.

About two weeks after the rumors started, while preparing to throw himself off The Golden Gate Bridge, Gerald Xavier Dongle used his cellphone to capture video of the thing causing the deaths. Gerald Xavier Dongle planned to throw himself off of the bridge because he happened to be a fabulously attired and obviously gay man of slight stature and build who was also named, unfortunately for him, Dongle, and who was living in an area that had been gay-friendly his whole life, but was now a playground for hate. He was out of his mind with terror.

Having climbed quite nimbly up one of the oxidized supports of the bridge, Mr. Dongle had a wonderful view, and he happened to have his phone with him, as he was about to text his last words to his partner. Though tortured by thoughts of his general plight in the world, and trembling with fear about his current plan to die by dropping several stories into the freezing bay, something about this new terror, when it caught his eye and he realized what it was, righted his mind so that he hit the icon for video instead of the one for text, and, when the image appeared on his screen, he managed to wrap his legs, supple from years of yoga, around the support and use one hand to steady the phone, while with the other he tapped record and zoomed in. It was still hard to make sense of the image that appeared on his screen and brought death to the families inside the mosque that morning due to the great degree of smoke surrounding it, but he could see the beast just fine with his eyes, and so as he showed the video to the San Francisco Police Department he described it in this way: a large flatbed truck fitted with not one, but ten smokestacks, rising up on either side of the flatbed like spider arms, sharp and pointy at the ends, and hissing forth huge belches of smog. The smog, he told them, seemed to be the culprit as neither the truck nor anyone on it touched the families in any way. It simply pulled up alongside the mosque, revved the engine, and toppled all as if they were mere paper dolls. The San Francisco Police Department immediately confiscated his phone, but Mr. Dongle had had the foresight to send the video to all of his friends and post it to his Facebook wall before coming nimbly down from his perch on the bridge.

Gerald Xavier Dongle was hailed a hero. Every morning show with a webcast booked him immediately. However, his first appearance was to be on *The Journal's* website the very next day. Mollie's friends gathered at her house. While chili finished cooking in a crockpot in the kitchen, the friends all crowded into her husband's basement office where there were two large computer monitors side-by-side on his desk, and readied themselves to watch Mr. Dongle show the world the evidence that would finally stop all this madness.

The live-stream began. Gerald Xavier Dongle turned-out to look quite a bit like pop-star Prince had during the *Purple Rain* days, causing quite a few of the women in Mollie's group, including Mollie herself, to regard him as very handsome, masculine, and heroic. *The Journal* had Mr. Dongle standing next to a large screen and narrating the phone video to explain the grey shapes. He had just paused the video to try to point out the details of the truck through the grey swirls of exhaust around it, when, quite surprisingly for all, a sniper bullet hit him in the head about an inch above the bridge of his nose.

The Journal pulled the livestream. The video from Mr. Dongle's phone was the next to go. Google alleged that the CIA had confiscated the phone from the police, and all copies of the video. Mr. Dongle's Facebook page was gone before Mollie and her neighbors had even stopped gasping. The truck, said the CIA on *Fox and Friends'* webpage in a taped interview, did not exist, and though it was unfortunate that Mr. Dongle was attacked so publicly, it had been his admitted intention to commit suicide, and so the hapless and obviously very disturbed man had gotten his wish: death and a lot of attention.

After that, though the mysterious deaths of large groups of people presumably continued, there was often no more than a whiff of it on the web. The Occupant was still MIA; The Running Mate was spending quality time with his family, and the country was being run by The Chairman of the Federal Reserve Bank, which was an appointment that was not prescribed in the Constitution, but which also made perfect sense, considering the country was so very capitalistic. The interest rates were now bouncing up and down like Slinkys to suit the corporations.

In the northeast, in the small coastal towns, the November beer, bottled some time before and just now ready to sip, was a cranberry wheat, for the upcoming Thanksgiving holiday. As she drove toward the New Hampshire state line on her way home from a twice-weekly teaching gig at the community college in the next state, Millie thought about picking up a six pack or two to share with the other moms and dads at her daughter's soccer game the next morning. She wasn't exactly sure of the protocol for tailgating at elementary school soccer, so she used the new handsfree voice-text app to message her husband and run the idea by him. Mollie had the voice function on her phone configured to "Mind-the-Gap Lady from the London Tube." She began to speak to Mollie:

Hello Honey. Great idea. I will pick up beers on bike after work. No problem. How were classes today?

Just as his message finished, Mollie yelled out, "Mother fucker!" The hands-free sent it to her husband.

Was it something I said? her husband's response came. As usual he was not at all surprised by her profanity.

"Just a damn seafood truck in front of me. Stopped for no reason. Now my phone and the entire contents of my purse are on the floor. Dammit!"

You okay? That last bit came through garbled. You were stopped for treason? And at worse you're on the floor?

"No," Mollie yelled in the general direction of where her phone had landed, "for no reason a truck in front of me stopped. Yeah I'm okay, just pulling over a minute. I'm fine."

Yep, no fine? That's good. We can buy more beer then.

"Wait, the voice recognition isn't hearing me right."

Okay, sure we can talk tonight. Bye sweetheart.

"Okay, whatever, bye."

"Aw, shit." With an exasperated sigh Mollie unbuckled, opened her door, walked around to the other side of her car, opened that door, and began to scoop the contents of her purse back into the leather bag. Purse zipped shut and safely back on her seat, the last thing she reached for was her phone, jammed up into the corner of the floor. She wiggled it loose, and stood upright. She went to close the passenger door, but somehow she missed the doorframe and lost her balance for a second, which caused her to drop her phone on the ground where it hit the asphalt with a dull thud.

"Shit," she said, slamming the door shut and bending at the waist to reach her phone. She turned it over in her palm as she righted herself. It seemed fine.

She returned to the driver's seat, buckled in, and dialed up a podcast on the phone. When she hit PLAY, a little crack appeared under her finger in the phone's screen. "Well, just a little crack; that's okay." She checked the rear-view, saw no cars on the road, and started back on her drive. Her podcast stopped playing. "Shit." She grabbed the phone and quickly tapped PLAY again. Another little crack spidered out from under her finger. The podcast stopped.

"Dammit!" said Mollie. She looked around the scenery to check for cops; there were none, so she quickly looked down again at the phone in her hand. She noticed her hand was shaking, which seemed odd to her. Maybe the car was riding rough. She hit PLAY and looked in her mirrors quickly to check the scene. She did a double-take because the road, about three or so miles back, looked as if it was covered in a dust cloud. It reminded Mollie of when they cut the cornfields when she was a kid. Those dried stalks made a lot of dust when the blades hit them, and Mollie loved the scent. She had always wanted to run behind, sniffing the dust deep into her lungs.

Still, now would be a rotten time to get stuck behind farm equipment, so she set the cruise control for fifty-eight mph, and tried again to start the podcast. What started playing instead was a recording she had made of herself singing to a karaoke track. She was not displeased with how good she sounded, but she really wanted the podcast back on, so she tried again to take a look at her phone. As there was no one else on the road, and she was on cruise control, she felt safe to let her knee hold the steering wheel while she tried to get her touch screen going.

Each time she hit PLAY the podcast would pick up where it left-off, and more cracks would appear in the screen. Mollie was on her eighth time touching PLAY when it occurred to her to check the road. She was still alone in front; the crab truck long since had left her in the dust. She was still driving fairly straight in her lane. But when she checked the rearview, well, the soot, the exhaust or smoke or whatever it was, was closer now, wasn't it? Wasn't it? Only about two miles away? She thought she could make out the outlines of a truck cab. She looked at her speedometer, and it was still doing fifty-eight. She scanned the world for cops, and upped her cruise speed, one, two, three, and she kept going, up to sixty-seven. She looked nervously in her mirror, then at her phone, and pressed PLAY again, and the screen gave out in cracks under her thumb like a fireworks display. She heard her own voice singing "Crazy."

"Dammit!"

She looked in her rearview. The dust cloud was closer, and she could clearly see a large truck cab, like an eighteen wheeler, through the belching exhaust. She tried to text her husband back, just to complain about her screen and maybe tell him about how the truck looked behind her, but her phone only brought up the game her daughter liked to play, decorating virtual cake pops.

She looked in her rearview mirror. It was definitely a truck, and it was definitely closer. Why was it kicking up so much dust? She checked the road ahead, and then squirmed around in her car to look at the truck over her shoulder. From this position she was able to see the spider legs, five on each side of the flat bed sticking their long nasty pointed selves up into the air. She could see that the dust or exhaust or whatever it was coming not from under the truck, but from those ten evil legs.

"Oh my fucking God, that's Dongle's goddamn truck," she said softly to herself. She looked at the roads signs. One sign said it was fifteen miles to the brewery in town, just four blocks from her house, her husband, her daughter, the dog.

"Oh my God, that's *the* truck!" She whacked at the phone's screen with her thumb, only to drop it with a shriek. A shard of the screen had jabbed into her skin. Her thumb was bleeding. Her phone was useless.

She stuck her thumb in her mouth, and tried to manipulate the cruise control with her other hand. She looked in the rearview. The truck was closing the distance between them somehow. She had to get home.

"Fuck this!" She cancelled the cruise controlled and hit the gas pedal hard. The needle topped eighty-five in about thirty seconds. When she checked her six, the grey smog was ahead of the truck, and right on top of her. It was like the smoke itself was chasing her. How could the exhaust be in front of the truck? Little particles in the smoke began pelting the back windscreen. The physics was all wrong. It should be getting pulled back by the truck's drag. She looked down at her speed. In her youth she had topped one-hundred many times, driving her friends up through the Vermont hills to get to the secret lake just outside Montpelier. She pressed the accelerator to the floor. She heard a popping sound, like her daughter squeezing a bag of chips to open them, using the air pressure to pop the seal. She looked in the rearview. A tiny crack was there in the previously perfect glass of the back windscreen. It was about the length of her thumb, and she had small fingers. Time to worry? The truck seemed closer, but so was the object of her eyes: now she saw only the windscreen clearly, both in her rearview and over her shoulder; the truck and the exhaust it belched became blurred background around it. The crack was only small, like her thumb. She checked her speed—103. She checked her six in the rearview. The crack appeared to wriggle, to move; it began to spiderweb. Here it split into three little tributaries; there it made four. It was very pretty, but she wondered if the insurance would cover it. She wondered why the physics was all wrong.

She checked the GPS. Ten miles to home. She looked at the back windscreen over her shoulder, craning her neck. There, by a split of five cracks, a little chunk of glass, about the size of a sunflower kernel, had fallen out. A little trickle of grey flowed through the hole like water. It seemed innocent, but it made the blood in her arteries sing danger in her ears. Another little pop, and the tentacles of the original crack spread farther.

She had to get home.

She saw more grey sneaking in when she glanced at the rearview. She felt heady, confused. She looked up ahead. She rubbed her eyes. At four miles from home there would be a stop sign. The GPS agreed. Four more miles. She would turn right, quickly, and floor it. She would lose the truck.

She could see it. It was there, up ahead. She could see it. The red octagon. Or was it a pentagon? The rearview was getting a grey film on it. But the front windshield was still clear, and the stop sign was coming toward her. She felt very light and very heavy at the same time. The stop sign was rushing toward her; it was trying to get to her, and she was having a new plan. When she got close to it, she would grab the pole, leap from the car, swing around it like her daughter on the monkey bars. She would drop to the ground on the balls of her feet, and spring into a run. The car would go straight; the truck would follow it, and she would run home and save everyone.

The stop sign was getting closer, but the grey smoke was curling through the broken windscreen and getting in her eyes like stray bangs. She brushed it away impatiently. The sign was not waiting. It was coming right toward her. It knew she intended to trick the belching truck.

The car was going to go straight on down the road . . .

The car was going to go straight on down the road. . .

The car was going to go straight on down the road. It was a good car. She would slip from it like a breath from a babe. Sweet and quiet. A little sigh escaping from a gap by the door hinge. The sign was so close now. Her legs were heavy heavy people; they pressed her down into the seat, pressed her feet together as one against the accelerator as if it was a radiator. Her feet were freezing cold now. Her heavy plodding legs did not like her plan. They were all earth, all grounded. They thought they could outrun the truck. Her head told them straight-up, *no, the physics are all wrong. You have to come with us. Look, the stop sign is going to help. It's all figured.*

Her head was like pure air. It knew things her legs didn't. The sign was so very close now. Her head was mellow, wispy, wise. *You cannot outrun the wheels because you have none.* Her legs would have to listen. Her mind was sharp and clean, like glass. The sign was heading right for her. She was heading right for it. The car would go straight. She could see it all so clear. The sign was right there. The gritty fog burned. She closed her big green eyes, and opened wide her arms.

GHOUL AND JACK

Ghoul and Jack
went to a shack
to fetch a pail of plasma.
Ghoul reclined
and broke her spine
and Jack developed asthma.

A HOME FOR THE INCURABLES

Bayne Northern

THE PUSTULES FIRST APPEARED THREE weeks ago. She found them in her razor-shaved armpit. She was itching and began scratching. Her fingernails grazed, then punctured, and finally invaded the small swellings. The chronic itching was driving her insane. Relief was only achieved when the warm goo of the pustules oozed over the tips of her fingers. She pulled her hand out of her shirt then examined the yellowish, milky substance, which slowly rolled down her digits. The fluid flowed freely in the little wrinkle lines just developing on her slender, manicured hands. She was grateful that the itching had finally stopped, but frustrated that it had been replaced with a painful, burning sensation. The first week the pustules appeared only around her armpits. The second week saw a rapid expansion. Little, pink, sore mounds began rising on her inner arms, then the inside of her thighs. When they began popping up all over her face, Amanda could no longer tolerate it. Although she hated going to the doctor to be poked and prodded, she didn't want to walk around town sporting the appearance of a pimply faced adolescent who appeared to be living off greasy burgers and fries.

Amanda's doctor raised her arm to closely examine the cluster of pus-filled polyps. He squinted with his right eye; his left eye was covered by a black eye patch. As Amanda looked up at his face, she thought he resembled a pirate. The doctor gently squeezed the raised, reddened bumps with his latex-gloved hands. As he did, he noticed the snail trails of scabs and dried blood caused by self-mutilation.

"How long have you had these?" he asked.

"About three weeks. They started in my armpit, then spread down my arms. Next, my inner thighs. As you can see, they're now exploding on my face."

The physician studied her with his one wet, watery blue eye which exuded a kindness and caring for mankind. Amanda always wondered why an individual would want to help people he didn't know. Why he was willing to inspect disgusting, sometimes putrid, physical symptoms associated with illness, injuries, and disease. She could never have done that with her life. If Amanda had to take care of the sick it would be every man for himself.

"I'm very perplexed. You're the tenth patient I've seen this week with these exact same symptoms. I've taken cultures and sent them to the lab. The results have all come back as *cause of bacterial infection unknown*. I've referred folks to dermatologists, prescribed antibacterial ointments and various antibiotics. None of these remedies has stopped the development of the purulent pimples causing so much pain and discomfort."

Amanda pursed her lips and uttered a low, deep moan.

"I'm suffering as well. This damn eye infection just won't clear up." He swiftly pulled the black patch up over his left eyebrow, exposing a pink, puffy orb with dried mucus dotting his lashes, and a wet, yellowish secretion oozing from his tear duct.

"That's not encouraging!" Amanda suddenly realized she was glowering at the doctor she had just met. She hoped like hell he wasn't contagious. She chastised herself for not signing up with a primary care physician when they were still accepting new patients. All local practices were now closed.

"Well, let me take a culture of a few of these. It'll sting a little bit."

He carefully swabbed a few of the pustules, slipping the contaminated cotton tips into small, clear tubes. He abruptly snapped the lid closed.

"I'll send these to a new lab. Maybe a different pathologist will be able to determine the cause. I'll also prescribe a corticoid ointment. It will give you some relief from the itching. Unfortunately, it won't inhibit further spreading of the rash."

"Whatever!" Amanda sounded like the teenager she'd been over 20 years ago.

Later that evening Amanda met up her best friends at the new High and Bye Nitrous Bar. They sat in a booth that had six different tubes coming out of the tops of the seats. The women paid $6.00 each to purchase a personal nasal cuff, selecting from navy, red, hot pink, black, and neon orange colors. They each slid the nasal cuff over the clear plastic tubing, ensuring to align it over the two little holes in the middle of the two-and-a-half-foot slender cylinder.

A waitress walked over to their booth and beamed a big, welcoming smile.

"How many nips of nitrous would you like to purchase this evening? The first nip costs $12. Subsequent nips are $8 each. The maximum number of nips is ten per person. Each nip will last about ten minutes. Customers must be at least 21 years of age and are required to wait ten minutes in between nips."

She pulled out a tablet to take their order.

"And, I recommend that you snort your nips simultaneously. It's more fun that way!"

The women ordered eight rounds. The ten-minute wait time between nips was perfect. Just as the buzz of a nitrous nip was dissipating, they could quickly rise back to the level of elation or "nip high" previously achieved. Amanda and her friends were thrilled with the faux exhilaration. They were laughing at each other, pointing at the little rubber nose cuffs on each of their faces. They looked ridiculous but felt great! They were now beautiful–strong–with positive outlooks on life. They were empowered, invincible superwomen–at least for an hour or so. Whoever conceived the idea of a nitrous bar was a genius. It was a great way to get high without inhaling carcinogens, consuming calories, or becoming impaired while visiting the bar.

Amanda was excited to return to the bar the following week to meet Jessica.

"Hey, girlfriend! Over here!" Jessica waved. She had already grabbed a seat at the nitrous nook, a six-seater booth equipped with six tubes.

Amanda gasped when she saw her friend. Jessica was pretty–in a ginger kind of way–like the Brittney Snow in *Pitch Perfect*. She had long, thick, wavy, auburn-colored hair which caused Amanda intense hair envy. Her large, oval, light-blue eyes were framed by long, dark, auburn lashes enhanced by Maybelline 5X mascara. A light peach, creamy complexion contributed to her healthy and vibrant look. Jessica was also blessed with a perfectly proportioned Barbie Doll figure. God had been kind to Jessica–she'd been given the total package. But Jessica didn't look vibrant and healthy that day.

The young women typically greeted each other with a big hug and a peck on the cheek. This time they both avoided those pleasantries like the plague.

"Jessica, oh, my God! It's happening to you, too!"

Amanda's mouth dropped wide open as she inspected her friend's face which was covered in open, oozing sores. Some of them had obviously cracked, drained a watery fluid for a period of time, and dried up. A mustard-colored, crusty coating speckled with little black dots of dried blood covered the abscesses.

Jessica looked down and started to cry.

"On, no! I hate crying. The tears sting these skin lesions on my face. They're already painful! The little droplets literally just add salt to the wound! I've been to my PCP and a dermatologist! I even went to Penn in Philly for additional testing but no one can figure it out! The only positive thing–and this isn't really positive but falls into the category of misery loves company–is that apparently a lot of folks in Sea Tree Beach have started to erupt with these skin lesions. At least you and I aren't the only ones!"

"I have a kind of skin lesion." Amanda tilted her face so that her right cheek was facing up, exposing the reddened, pock-marked, and bumpy surface. "They're called pustules–puss-filled pimples. They started in my pits, continued down my arms, my thighs, and now my face. No medical test has been able to determine the cause or identify the cure. I feel like a leper! Together, we could start a leper colony!"

The two women instinctively hugged each other–burying their faces in their shoulders, weeping softly, and commiserating over their mutual maladies.

"Let's order a nip!" suggested Amanda enthusiastically. "That will make us feel better. We can at least have one nip before our other friends arrive. They'll understand why we went ahead when they take one look at us!"

The women shook their heads in agreement and chuckled.

"I'll take the black nasal cuff and you take the orange one. It's almost Halloween after all!" Jessica pushed the rubber, orange nose cone over to Amanda. Then, she gently slid the black one onto the clear tubing, being careful to center the nasal cuff over the two little holes. Her friend quickly followed her lead. They waved the waitress over, happily ordering their first nip of the night. In a few moments both had a wonderful sensation that all was well with the world. They felt content and complacent. Soon, they were laughing hysterically, entertaining each other, describing the onset of their skin diseases, the attempts to cure it, and subsequent attempts to conceal it.

The girls were so engrossed in their conversations that they were startled when they looked up. Their other three friends were standing by their nook, observing them with wide-eyed stares. As Amanda and Jessica raised their eyes, their expressions morphed into absolute astonishment.

They watched in horror as Hayley plucked little wiggly worms out of small toothpick-sized holes in her arms. She dropped the off-white, squiggly insects onto the floor and carefully planted her shoe on top of a pile of them. She moved her foot in a circular motion, slowly grinding the maggot mound into a pulpy mush on the bar-room floor. Hayley made a mental note to clean her shoe when she got home.

"What are those?" Amanda leaned way back to avoid any contact with Hayley's extremities.

"Worms! And, nobody knows how I got them or how to treat them. They are driving me insane! I normally wear my long sleeves down. I just had to roll them up and pluck a couple of these little buggers off! I could feel their heads popping in and out of the small tunnels in my arms. It was driving me nuts!"

"Gross!" exclaimed Amanda and Jessica in unison.

"I could say the same about the two of you!" Hayley quickly rolled her sleeves back down. "What's the matter with your mugs?"

As the girls exchanged horror stories, Tara and Melanie excused themselves to slip into the ladies room. Hayley slid into the

113

booth, making sure there was enough room for the other two when they returned from the restroom.

Amanda noticed that Tara's left arm was dragging by her side when she walked across the room and returned to the booth. Her limb appeared lifeless. It was swinging around independently as if it didn't belong to her body. She also noticed that Melanie had lost weight. She looked pale and pallid. She was hunched over, apparently in some kind of abdominal distress.

"What's going on with the two of you?" Jessica asked as they slid into the nook. Each of them chose a nasal cuff and adeptly slid it on one of the last two remaining tubes.

"My left arm is dead–paralyzed somehow. I've had a barrage of tests. No one can determine the cause or the cure. I'm scheduled to go to Johns Hopkins next week for another round of medical trials. Thank god I'm right handed! Let's order some nips!" Tara waved enthusiastically at the wait staff with her good arm.

Melanie admitted, "I could really use a hit right now. I've been overcome by chronic diarrhea. That's why I made sure I got the end seat on the booth–in case I need to make a run for it!" She sighed loudly.

"Same as you guys. Seen multiple specialists to no avail. Nothing is working. My insides are just pouring out! It's awful! It's ruining the quality of my life!"

The young women nodded in agreement, acknowledging their respective predicaments. The nitrous nips really helped bring levity to their dire situations. They talked through the evening, speculating about the cause of the infections. They discussed where they had been, what they had eaten, any unusual contact they had had. Nothing seemed to pop out as a common theme among them. They agreed that Sea Tree Beach's reputation was evolving from a family and gay-friendly, quaint little beach town to a home for the incurables. The women stayed very late, only leaving after the nitrous tap last call.

As weeks passed culminating into months, each of the women continued to undergo a battery of medical tests. A large percentage of the local population had been infected with different diseases. The sick no longer had to drive to Philly or Baltimore, or fly to Chicago to be seen by top-rated specialists in their fields. The medical experts now came to them. A special triage was set up in the Sea Tree Beach Firehouse for those deemed to be in critical condition. Physicians and pathologists conducted all kinds of medical tests and trials in its former garage.

Wildlife and environmental experts and scientists were also roaming throughout the town, taking samples of Sea Tree Beach's water, sand, and dirt. Animals indigenous to the area were captured, tranquilized, weighed, and measured. Syringes of bodily fluids were drawn and then the creatures were released back into the wild. Many theories regarding the cause of the incurable diseases required growing organisms in petri dishes. As a result, it was taking months to examine each hypothesis. In most cases, every single hypothesis was wrong.

Until the day one wasn't.

The cause of the infections was eventually identified by a well-regarded shark biologist named Gary White. White theorized that the completed $50 million Sea Tree Beach sewage project was altering the natural environment. The new system pushed massive amounts of city sewage with high fecal bacteria concentration into the nearby Hen & Chicken Reef. White hypothesized that the substance was detrimentally impacting sea life. The Hen & Chicken Reef was considered a critical shark pupping area near the entrance to the bay. The biologist correctly surmised that the shark pups were ingesting high concentrations of fecal-infected water. The newborns were pumping the waste water over their gills and then excreting a high-intensity drug-resistant bacteria that normally resided in their guts. The *News Journal* ran an article summarizing White's study noting,

White and his team found significant amounts of drug-resistant bacteria in dozens of shark species. His team gathered and tested thousands of samples by swabbing their genital cavities. Staphylococcus, E. coli, and over 100 other types of microbes were impervious to naturally occurring antibiotics as well as synthetic drugs. The scientists found microorganisms in sharks that swam close to shore and far out to sea.

Apparently, the bacteria from shark guts significantly multiplied due to the high level of fecal bacteria dumped into the pup pools. Their germs were then released directly into the ocean water through shark defecation. All species of fish were inhaling their excrement through their gills. The cold-blooded aquatic vertebrates were caught, cleaned, and purchased by local restaurants. The eateries offered and advertised their daily, fresh-fish specials. Vacationers spending only one week in the beach town would typically not be infected. However, local residents who regularly consumed the contaminated seafood over several months eventually succumbed to a bacterial infection. The germs typically manifested themselves in the weakest part of the individual's body, creating a toxicity that ultimately developed into some kind of incurable illness. Frequently swimming in the Sea Tree Beach ocean water resulted in shark fecal flakes entering the body's orifices, providing an opportunity for the drug-resistant microbes to invade its human host.

Sea Tree Beach declared a national emergency and requested federal aid to clean the germ-infested waters. City officials closed the beaches, prohibited swimming, and banned fishing indefinitely in the coastal waters in an attempt to control further contamination.

Identifying the cause of the incurable diseases occurred three years after the first residents were initially afflicted. Potential cures were just starting to undergo rigorous, scientific studies. As their illnesses progressed, the stricken suffered. While the community awaited the results of the medical research, many of the early infected Sea Tree Beach inhabitants were irreversibly disfigured, permanently paralyzed, or died.

The Sea Tree Sands Hotel was no longer able to attract guests to the little beach town. The owners generously donated the facility to the city on the condition that the building be used solely to care for the incurables. Sea Tree Beach administrators immediately contracted the local hospital to oversee and manage the conversion of the hotel to a long-term medical facility. After eighteen months of renovation, it was completed and renamed The Sea Tree Sands Caring Community: A Home for the Incurables. At full capacity, it could house over two-hundred patients in its assisted-living facility and fifty in its skilled nursing unit.

The once-new, innovative, nitrous bar market had grown appreciably over the past few years during Sea Tree Beach's epidemic. Other nitrous bars had opened throughout the area. The High and

Bye Nitrous Bar was still a popular gathering place, but it now catered to a younger clientele. Another frequented nitrous bar was Puff and Stuff, known for both its sweet and spicy-flavored nips as well as its generous-sized pub food portions. The Nitrous Night Club attracted the more mature patrons, featuring early-bird specials of nips at half price and a private room for incurables. Gail's Inhale enticed customers with its comfy, slouchy sofas and overstuffed chairs. The newest, casual nitrous bar, Nip, Suck, and Shuck, located on the boardwalk, included nitrous tubes coiling out of the sides of the tables holding mounds of icy-fresh Cape May salt oysters.

Amanda and her friends gathered together at the Nitrous Night Club, their favorite nip bar, on the same date they were initially infected three years ago. They started to commiserate, but stopped complaining after huffing their first hit. They grabbed a few stools right across from the bartender. The women proceeded to inhale their nips from the tubular tentacles extending from behind the bar, laying across the narrow, laminated, mahogany counter.

Amanda and Jessica wore black, translucent burka-like scarves to hide their grotesquely, disfigured faces. Wearing burkas had become quite common in Sea Tree Beach as a result of the facial scarring caused by the bacterial infections. The two gently slid their nasal cuffs under and up the filmy, facial covering of their headdresses. The clear plastic tubes began to fill with a light mist, then quickly cleared as they each inhaled.

"A toast to the kind and caring hands of the Sands!" Tara raised her tube. A tear rolled down her check and bounced off her chin. "And, to all of us! The survivors!"

She waved her hand across the bar, then gracefully lowered her head in remembrance of those who had suffered and succumbed to death. Tara still had one good arm but *only* one arm; the other had been severed following the onset of gangrene. Tara's arm had swollen to almost double in size. Her skin had cracked and oozed a foul-smelling pus. Her flesh had turned dark green and then black. Pieces of her skin had started to peel. The pain had been unbearable. The physician had tried all kinds of antibiotics. Finally, he decided to amputate. Tara had a very positive attitude about it. She joked with the other women that the missing appendage took at least ten pounds off the scale. She had also nimbly mastered sliding the nasal cuff on the tube using just two fingers of her one, remaining hand.

"Here! Here!" Amanda and Jessica chimed in once again tapping their tubes together.

As the women breathed in deeply, they saw each other as they once were. They reminisced about the good times they once had together. But in talking about their escapades, their moods turned somber.

Tara, Amanda, and Jessica raised their tubes off the counter, lightly touched them together, and softly exclaimed in unison, "In memory of Melanie!" They remembered their good friend, who had starved to death at forty-two years of age. Her body, ravaged by years of abdominal distress, had become immune to absorbing and processing nutrients.

Their next nip was preceded with a plea for Hayley. She had just been accepted into the skilled nursing section of the Sea Tree Sands Caring Community. The maggots had spread through the worm tunnels, traveling up through her arms and into her torso, invading all of her major bodily organs. She had been diagnosed as incurable.

The toast to Hayley was initiated by the formerly agnostic Amanda. She had once viewed praying as a form of hedging—in case there was a God. Over time, she had become convinced there had to be a deity that could alleviate the pain and misery.

"We pray for the end of suffering for our friend, Hayley. We ask God to welcome our friend into the halls of heaven, granting her peace, joy, and life everlasting."

Tears trickled down all of their faces as they wished for their friend's death, her only possible escape from agony.

...WARMER AND CLEAR TOMORROW

David W. Dutton

JENNIFER MASON LIFTED THE KITCHEN curtain and stared out at the pea soup pressing thickly against the twelve-paned window. Beyond the blanket of fog, the buoy outside the harbor rang dismally as the long swells rolled in from the sea. Damn the fog! It meant only one thing to her. Mike, her husband, would not be home again tonight. In Boston for two days of meetings, he would now be stranded there, as the ferry to the island ceased operations until the fog lifted. Mike's absence also meant she would have to spend another night alone in the house. Jennifer supposed it was silly, but she hated being alone in the old house. It was too big, too full of shadows and dark corners.

"Well, Jennie, old girl, you're thirty-two years old. You've done it before, and you'll do it again. One more night won't matter."

Dropping the curtain, she poured herself another cup of coffee and sat down to the kitchen table. Maybe Millie would spend the night. But no, Millie's nine-year-old son, Tom, had the mumps, and Millie would need to stay with him. Oh well, it would soon be over, and Mike would be home. No more trips to Boston; at least not until next month.

Jennifer jumped as Millie slammed the kitchen door behind

her.

"They've found her!"

"Good God, Millie! You scared me to death!"

"Sorry." Millie slid into the chair across from her friend. "Tom's down with the mumps, but he'll be fine for a bit by himself. But I knew you'd want to know."

"Know what?" Jennifer set down her empty coffee mug.

"That they found the Aldridge girl!"

Jennifer's blank look caused Millie to pause.

"The Aldridge girl; the one who went missing last Friday."

Jennifer smiled. "Well, that's good news."

"No, it's not. They found her in the harbor. She's dead."

Jennifer looked stunned. "That's horrible."

Millie jumped from her chair and headed toward the kitchen door. "Come on. They're just now pulling her in."

"Millie! For heaven's sake, don't be morbid. I have no intention of going down there."

"Oh, come on. You've been cooped up in here long enough."

"I am not going down there. I hate when people stand around staring at someone else's misfortune."

"You've been shut up in this dreadful house ever since Mike left. You need a change if nothing else. Besides, it's not likely they're going to let us see the body."

Jennifer sighed. "Oh, all right." She grabbed her coat from a peg on the wall and followed Millie out into the fog. "Do you think this mess is going to lift?"

"Not any time soon. Certainly not in time for what you want."

Jennifer pulled the door closed behind them. Should she lock it? What was the point? This wasn't Boston, and she would be coming right back.

The fog cast a gray pall over everything. The air was damp against her skin as they walked toward the harbor. The bell buoy continued its dismal song.

In a matter of minutes, they were standing among a crowd of people perched on the rocks above the beach. Below them, men grappled in the water near an open boat to bring in the corpse.

Jennifer leaned close to Millie and kept her voice low. "I feel like an ass standing here like this."

Millie ignored her and kept her eyes riveted on the scene. "They've almost got her."

For some reason, Jennifer was scared. The feeling came suddenly and without warning. When they finally recovered the body, Jennifer followed the rest of the crowd onto the beach. She didn't want to be there. She didn't want to see the Aldridge girl, but she followed the crowd nonetheless.

It was a sight Jennifer would never forget. The coroner was leaning over the body, obscuring it from the sight of the crowd. Millie's gripped Jennifer's hand so tightly that it began to hurt. Suddenly, the coroner stood up, revealing the battered body of the young woman. A gasp escaped from the crowd. The jagged line along the front of the victim's throat was unmistakable. Whatever beauty Mary Aldridge may have once had was gone. She'd been in the water long enough for the crabs to do their disgusting work. Her eyes were gone, and her fingers and toes were picked clean. She had been nibbled upon in numerous other places, but these left no impression on Jennifer. The meatless fingers were enough. Jennifer stared in horror and then turned quickly away.

"A murder! Of all things! Right here in Snug Harbor."

Millie talked on as Jennifer stumbled silently along beside her. Her mind was filled with the image of those awful fingers.

Jennifer stopped suddenly and grabbed Millie's arm. "I forgot to lock the kitchen door!"

"What? With a murderer on the loose?"

Jennifer quickened her step. "I didn't *know* there was a murderer until a few minutes ago."

The house loomed suddenly out of the fog. The door was unlocked, and Jennifer did not want to be alone.

"Millie, ask me to lunch."

"But Tom has the mumps."

"I've had them already. Both sides."

Millie smiled as Jennifer locked the kitchen door. "Then consider yourself asked."

Jennifer toyed with the chicken salad sandwich and picked at the bowl of chips. She had no appetite. She kept seeing the fingers of the dead girl and hearing the bell ringing in the distance. Mike would be home tomorrow. That was all that mattered.

"Millie, will you spend the night at my place?"

"Oh honey, I wish I could, but with Tom with the mumps–"

"You're right. I was wrong to ask."

"Why don't you stay here? There's plenty of room."

Jennifer looked out the window at the fog and sighed. "I'm afraid that's out of the question. Mike's supposed to call, and if I'm not there, he'll be worried."

Cellular reception on the island was practically nonexistent, and most islanders depended on land lines for communication.

Jennifer spent the rest of the day at Millie's. She knew she should go home, but each time she looked out the window, she became more afraid of entering the big stone house. What awaited her there? Had the murderer entered during her absence?

Doubtful, but still possible. She was just being silly. She had to get a grip.

Jennifer and Millie whiled away the afternoon talking, carefully avoiding the subject that was foremost on their minds. Even Millie's normal chattiness seemed strained at times.

With a sigh, Jennifer glanced at her watch and rose from her chair.

"Goodness! It's almost five. I have to be getting home."

"Why don't you at least stay for supper?"

"Thanks, but Mike could call any time now. I need to be there."

Jennifer let herself out into the mist and started home. The big, stone house was almost lost in the fog, only a ghostly outline of gables and chimneys. Once, she stopped to look back at Millie's house where bright lights burned, but then trudged ahead toward the darkened windows of her own home. Hadn't she left on any lights? Surely, the kitchen light should be on. She would take care of that problem soon enough.

Jennifer entered the kitchen and switched on the ceiling light. There was only one light in the long, narrow room. It did little to brighten the gloom. She entered the dining room, switched on the chandelier and walked into the living room beyond where she lit every available lamp.

"Well, you really should eat something." It was better to hear her own voice than the silence that filled the house.

She opened the refrigerator door and had the half-gallon of milk in her hand when a sudden pounding at the kitchen door made her jump. As she spun around, the bottle slipped from her grasp and crashed to the floor. The white liquid flowed along the floor and seeped into the cracks of the tile.

"Mrs. Mason?" The pounding continued. "Mrs. Mason...you home? It's Charlie Simpkins, Neighborhood Watch."

Jennifer rushed to the door and opened it to face the red-haired young man standing on the stoop. "Oh, Charlie! I'm sorry... I just spilled a bottle of milk."

"Oh, sorry, ma'am. You okay? We're just going door to door checking on everyone."

"I guess you could say I'm a little spooked." She tried to laugh but failed.

"You and everyone else, ma'am. Want to be sure all your doors and windows are locked. The police don't have a clue as to this guy's whereabouts."

"You don't have to worry about that."

He smiled and turned to leave. "Well, you call 911 if you see or hear anything suspicious."

"I will. Thanks for checking on me."

Jennifer closed and locked the door and began cleaning up the mess she'd made. Once finished, she dismissed all thoughts of eating and retreated to the living room. The radio caught her eye. It would drown out the oppressive silence.

". . . warmer and clear tomorrow. Repeating our top story: The body of twenty-three-year old Mary Aldridge was found today floating in Snug Harbor. Her death was attributed to a severed juggler vein. No clues to the whereabouts of the murderer have . . ."

With one quick movement, Jennifer silenced the commentator. If only Mike would call. If only the fog would lift. She stood before one of the living room windows and nervously fingered her necklace. Oh Lord, let it lift. She drew back the curtain and looked out. A cat, that had sought refuge on the outside sill, jumped to the ground. Jennifer screamed, dropped the drape and covered her face with her hands. God, she was a mess!

"What you need is a drink." She turned to the liquor cabinet, found a half-full bottle of Merlot and filled one of the long-stemmed wine glasses. Her eyes fell on an open pack of Mike's cigarettes lying inside the cabinet. Why the hell not? She extracted one badly bent cigarette. As she lit it, she noticed that her hands were shaking.

Jennifer sat on the sofa, nervously sipping wine until the cigarette went out and was thrown into the fireplace. Suddenly the room was filled with the ringing of the phone. She quickly picked up the receiver.

"Mike? Oh, hi Millie. It thought it was Mike calling. No, not yet. I'm fine. No, I'd better wait for him to call. Thanks, again for today."

She replaced the receiver.

Mike didn't phone until nine o'clock. The fog was supposed to lift, but he doubted he would get home tonight. Yes, he had heard about the murder. Be sure all the windows and doors were locked, and don't go out of the house. No, not even to Millie's. He would be home as soon as possible. He loved her.

"Be sure all the windows and doors are locked. Oh, God!" Systematically, she made the rounds of the ground floor, locking and checking the doors and windows. At the foot of the rear staircase, she stopped and looked up at the darkness. She reached for the light switch. Nothing happened.

"Damn!"

She flicked the switch again. It was no use.

Slowly, Jennifer mounted the stairs. She crept up one at a time, glancing every so often behind her. The tall, case clock on the landing struck the hour. Startled, Jennifer slipped and only saved herself by grabbing the railing. It took all the courage she could summon to continue the climb into darkness. At the top of the stairs, she hesitated and then ran into the master bedroom. Flicking on the overhead light, she glanced nervously around the room. All was in order. She turned to the other two rooms off the front hall. They, too, were secure. She left the lights burning and reentered the master bedroom. Her task was not yet complete. She stepped into the back hall and glanced down the stairs. Was someone there? No, it was just a shadow cast by the clock on the landing. You're being foolish, she told herself.

Now, there was only the bath and one bedroom, but she would have to cross the wide expanse of the bedroom to reach

Mike's study at the rear of the house. She just wouldn't bother, but she damn well better. The whole rear wing was bounded by the porch–a perfect means of entrance to the second floor.

The bathroom window was locked as were those in the bedroom. When she opened the door to the study, the dampness closed around her. She turned on the light.

"Oh, God!" It was more of a prayer this time.

None of the windows were locked–they were all open. She ran from window to window, all the while cussing Mike for having left them this way. With the windows closed and locked, she started down the servants' stairs and remembered all the lights she had left burning. Mike would have a fit if she left them all on.

Quickly, she retraced her steps, switching off lights as she went. Deciding to leave the light burning in the master bedroom, she turned to leave. As she did, she caught sight of the attic door. The attic! She glared at the narrow, crooked door. The wooden toggle held the door firmly in place. No one was coming through there.

Without glancing behind her, she ran down the front stair to the living room. The living room, however, was less comforting than she thought it would be. She kept looking at the heavily draped windows, the shadowy corners, and the darkness beyond the entry hall. With a sigh, Jennifer sat on the sofa and picked up her wine glass. The thick, red liquid was soothing to her throat. She leaned her head against the back of the sofa. It was after eleven when she fell asleep.

It was foggy out. She was going to meet Mike at the ferry terminal. From the car, she could barely see the lights from the little wooden structure. Mike had told her to wait and to make sure all the doors and windows were locked. It was five minutes or so before she could see someone walking to her out of the fog. She recognized Mike's old trench coat. She unlocked the door, and he got in. Before he leaned over to kiss her, Jennifer removed his hat. Her eyes met only the sightless sockets of Mary Aldridge. She screamed as it reached out to touch her. The bones of the hand caressed her cheek as she screamed again.

She was crying now, sobbing hysterically. The nightmare had been too real. Those fingers. God, those awful fingers. It was some time before she stopped crying and gained her self-control. She hated the thought of going to bed, but she couldn't sit there all night. Walking to the foot of the front stairs, she could see the light from the master bedroom burning confidently. Jennifer gave up and climbed the stairs.

Once in bed, she found it hard to sleep. She left the bedside lamp burning, but the doors to the closets bothered her. As long she and Mike had lived there, the closet doors hadn't closed properly. In the dimness of the room, they seemed to open wider and wider.

Jennifer sat up and pulled the thin bed curtains closed on the Victorian canopy bed. There! No more closet doors to watch. She turned on her side and dragged the comforter up and under her chin. It was quite some time before sleep finally came.

Jennifer sat up quickly. Something had awakened her, but the house was silent now except for the ticking of the bedside clock. It was 2:40 AM. There it was again . . . a subtle scratching sound. Suddenly, in the dim light from the lamp, a form began to take shape. She watched as the form moved toward the left side of the bed. It began to fumble with the bed curtains, pawing at the gap where the curtains met. Oh God! Jennifer's breath was coming is short gasps. She slowly slid to the other side of the big bed, still watching the shadowy form. As she gazed in horror, it found the curtain gap. One boney finger pierced the gap followed by three more. Then the other hand grabbed one edge of the curtain and began to pull it back. Jennifer screamed. At the sound, the form gripped both curtains and pulled them roughly aside. She stared into Mary Aldridge's sightless eyes and screamed again.

Jennifer rolled off the bed, onto the floor, entangled in the bed curtains. On hands and knees, she fought the yards of fabric until she was free. Quickly she crawled across the room, too afraid to look behind her. When she reached the door to the back hall, Jennifer grabbed the casing and pulled herself to her feet. Oh God! She dared to glance back into the room. The horrible form had moved away from the bed and stood midway between Jennifer and the foot of the bed. A puddle of water encircled its feet. Jennifer gasped and stepped through the doorway. Tears ran down her cheeks.

Oh God, help me! Slowly, the form raised one arm and reached out toward Jennifer. The boney index finger curled back in a slow, come-hither motion. Jennifer screamed and ran down the rear stairway. In her haste, her feet became entangled in her long night-gown, and she pitched forward. Jennifer reached for the railing but missed it as she lost her balance and fell. In panic, she grasped one of the stair spindles, but her weight, coupled with the force of her fall, caused the spindle to break.

She fell head-long down the stairway, hitting her head on the base of the case clock on the landing. Darkness closed around her.

Where was she? God, she hurt. Her neck was in a peculiar position, and her head pounded. What had happened? She fought the need to open her eyes. Not yet. Give it a minute. Something was very wrong.

With the sudden realization, Jennifer's eyes flew open. Mary Aldridge! Oh God! Jennifer stared up the shadowy stairway. The hallway above was empty. Had it been a dream? No. It was too real for that. An apparition? She didn't know; she didn't want to know.

Suddenly, Jennifer noticed the bright light to her left. She had left the dining room chandelier burning, but its soft glow was now eclipsed by a brighter source. The sun poured through the big bay window and cast a myriad of patterns on the oriental carpet. The sun. Oh thank God, the sun!

Jennifer grasped the newel post and pulled herself to her feet. She ached. She rubbed the large bump on the back of her head. After pausing for a moment she descended the two steps from the landing to the dining room. Jennifer grasped the back of a dining chair and guided herself toward the bay window. In one, quick move, she collapsed on the Victorian sofa in the bay window and rested her chin on its carved back. Outside, the sun was indeed shining, bathing her garden in a multitude of color. She sighed and closed her eyes. The sun felt so good on her face.

Beyond the harbor, the doleful tolling of the bell buoy had been replaced by a new sound. The wind that had driven away the fog had set up a chop that caused the bell to ring happily. It was a new day, and Mike would soon be home.

Behind her, a small trickle of sea water crept down the stairs, and a skeletal hand reached out to grab the polished banister.

CONTRIBUTOR BIOS

CRANDELL

William F. Crandell returned home from the Vietnam War with a taste for adventure, a skeptic's eye, and a hundred thousand stories. Completing a doctorate in history at Ohio State University, he was awarded a Maryland State Arts Council Individual Artist Award in 2004 for his mystery novel, *Let's Say Jack Kennedy Killed the Girl*. Bill has published numerous short stories, book reviews, and political analyses. He was awarded the PRIZM's Mark Twain Award for Humor/Social Commentary 2012 and resides in Milton with his wife, Judith.

DUTTON

David W. Dutton is a semi-retired residential designer who was born and raised in Milton, DE. He has written two novels, several short stories, and eleven plays. His musical comedy, *oh! Maggie*, in collaboration with Martin Dusbiber, was produced by the Possum Point Players and the Lake Forest Drama Club. He wrote two musical reviews for the Possum Point Players: *An Evening With Cole Porter*, in collaboration with Marcia Faulkner, and *With a Song in My Heart*. He also wrote the one-act play, *Why the Chicken Crossed the Road*, commissioned and produced by the Delmarva Chicken Festival. In 1997, he was awarded a fellowship as an established writer by the Delaware Arts Council. In 1998, he received a first-place award for his creative nonfiction by the Delaware Literary Connection. His piece, "Who is Nahnu Dugeye?" was subsequently published in the literary anthology, Terrains. In conjunction with the Milton Workshop, he is completing his third novel, *One of the Madding Crowd*. David, his wife, Marilyn, and their Rottweiler, Molly, currently reside in Milton.

LEWES

TJ Lewes had a fascinating bio, full of intrigue and mystery, but it vanished one stormy evening in October and was never seen again. Foul play is suspected.

NORTHERN
After publishing the Executive Summary to "The Future of Independent Life Insurance Distribution," Bayne Northern transitioned from writing nonfiction to fiction. She is currently completing her first novel, *The Bitch Seat*, situated in the financial services industry. An avid short story author, Bayne is also an active volunteer of the Village Improvement Association, a resident of Rehoboth Beach, and a proud owner of Thatcher, the corgi.

PEARCE
Dianne Pearce founded The Milton Workshop. She is a graduate of both the West Chester University and Vermont College writing programs, earning an MA and an MFA. Dianne has taught writing in Delaware, California, Pennsylvania, and Maryland. She sometimes takes on editing projects for other writers, and has done both writing and advocacy for causes close to her heart, among them adoption, developmental disabilities, and animals. Dianne loves living in Milton, and claims to have read *Paradise Lost* in her youth, the real version where all the S-es look like Fs, which she says must count for something.

POLO
Mark Alan Polo has been an interior designer for over 30 years and is President and Owner of The Urban Dweller/Polo M.A. Inc., with offices in Northern New Jersey and a satellite office in Delaware. Mark became a permanent Delaware resident in 2014. A part-time writer for the past 15 years, Mark's recent short story, "Fifty-Five," appeared in the 2016 award-winning *Beach Nights* anthology (Cat and Mouse Press). His debut novel, *Mosquitos and Men*, is slated for publication in 2018. He is at work on a second novel.

SPEIZER CRANDELL
Judith Speizer Crandell is an award-winning writer and teacher of fiction, poetry, and nonfiction. She's received residencies at Yaddo, AROHO (A Room of One's Own), and a Maryland State Arts Council Individual Artist Fellowship for her novel, *The Resurrection of Hundreds Feldman*. She has performed readings at the New York State Writers Institute, the New York State Vietnam Veterans Memorial and the Washington, DC, and Cleveland Public Libraries. A journalist

and Washington, DC, speechwriter for nearly 20 years, she moved to Milton, DE, in July to be near the ocean and write.

YURKOVICH

Milton-based author David is the 2017 Delaware Division of the Arts fellow (emerging talent) in the category of literature. David began writing in 1992 with a focus on graphic novels and comics. His first self-published comic was funded by a grant by the Xeric Foundation. As a writer and illustrator, his works include *Death by Chocolate* and *Less Than Heroes* (both published by Top Shelf Productions) and *Altercations* (published by Sleeping Giant). In 2007 David wrote, designed, and published *Mantlo: A Life in Comics*, a benefit magazine to help aid in the medical expenses of Bill Mantlo (creator of Rocket Raccoon and other Marvel Comics properties). In 2016, David was among 10 prose authors statewide selected to attend the Delaware Seashore Poetry & Prose Writers' Retreat. His short story, "The Last Day of Summer," appeared in the 2016 anthology *Beach Nights* (Cat and Mouse Press). He has published two prose novels, *Glass Onion* and *Banana Seat Summer*, with two manuscripts in development. Most recently, David provided an introduction to the second volume of the *Deadly Hands of Kung Fu Omnibus*, published 2017 by Marvel.